His eyes held hers. 'Did you get my messages?'

'Yes. But I didn't want to speak to you.' She shrugged. 'I still don't, Lord Arnborough.'

His mouth twisted. 'It's just a title, Joanna. I'm still the same man.'

'Rubbish,' she spat at him with sudden heat. 'You're the umpteenth Baron Arnborough. And I assume the "sort of flat" you live in is a suite of apartments roped off from the public at the Hall. No wonder you laughed when I said I'd like to marry the heir.'

'All right, Joanna. If you mean that, there's nothing more to say. I am who I am. Thank you for supper. Again. I'll be on my way.'

Jo leapt up in consternation. 'No. Please. Don't go yet.'

'Why not?'

She glared in him resentfully. 'You could at least try a little more persuasion.'

Suddenly very still, March raised an unsettling eyebrow. 'If I do resort to persuasion, Miss Logan, it might not be to your taste.'

'Try me.'

Catherine George was born in Wales, and early on developed a passion for reading which eventually fuelled her compulsion to write. Marriage to an engineer led to nine years in Brazil, but on his later travels the education of her son and daughter kept her in the UK. And, instead of constant reading to pass her lonely evenings, she began to write the first of her romantic novels. When not writing and reading she loves to cook, listen to opera, and browse in antiques shops.

Recent titles by this author:

†THE ITALIAN COUNT'S DEFIANT BRIDE
*CHRISTMAS REUNION
THE MILLIONAIRE'S REBELLIOUS MISTRESS
THE MILLIONAIRE'S CONVENIENT BRIDE
THE RICH MAN'S BRIDE

†Part of *International Billionaires*
*In the anthology *Married by Christmas*

THE MISTRESS
OF HIS MANOR

BY
CATHERINE GEORGE

First published in Great Britain 2009
Harlequin Mills & Boon Limited,
Eton House, 18-24 Paradise Road, Richmond, Surrey TW9 1SR

© Catherine George 2009

ISBN: 978 0 263 87457 0

Set in Times Roman 10¼ on 11¼ pt
01-1209-54631

Harlequin Mills & Boon policy is to use papers that are natural, renewable and recyclable products and made from wood grown in sustainable forests. The logging and manufacturing process conform to the legal environmental regulations of the country of origin.

Printed and bound in Spain
by Litografia Rosés, S.A., Barcelona

THE MISTRESS
OF HIS MANOR

CHAPTER ONE

Low afternoon sunlight was so dazzling after the gloom of the grafting house he fished dark glasses from a pocket as he walked past the potting sheds and greenhouses to skirt a virtual traffic jam of loaded trolleys on the main concourse. Excellent. Business was good. Even better, one of the trolleys was manned by a very attractive girl. He heaved a sigh as two men joined her, one of them holding a toddler by the hand. Damn. Not single, then. And years younger than her husband. Lucky dog. As he drew level the girl gave him a smile that stopped him in his tracks.

'Could you give us directions, please? We need winter-flowering pansies.'

'Of course. I'll take you there,' he said promptly. Or anywhere she wanted.

'Thank you.' She bent to kiss the child's cheek. 'You go with Daddy and Grandpa, poppet.'

'Come with *you*,' the little girl said mutinously.

'Darling, you're a bit hot, and it will be even hotter where the pansies live, so ask Daddy to buy you an ice cream.'

The magic words sent the child towards her father, beaming.

'I'll meet you all at the main entrance afterwards,' called the mother, and turned to her guide. 'Right—sorry to keep you hanging about.'

'No problem at all,' he assured her, and led her on a shame-lessly roundabout route. Her husband could spare her for a minute or two, he told his conscience. When they finally reached the colourful display of pansies he commandeered an empty trolley and took his customer on a conducted tour.

She gave him the smile again. 'How beautiful. You have the most gorgeous plants here.'

'You come here often?' Hell—couldn't he have come up with something better than that?

'No. First visit. My mother trusted pansy selection to me. She wants every shade of pink on offer, plus yellow and white.'

'No violet?' he said, surprised.

'Apparently not. Thank you for your help,' she added, 'but you must be busy. I can manage now.'

'I can spare a few minutes.' Or hours. 'You choose; I'll load up.'

He eyed her covertly as she made her choice, sure he'd seen her somewhere before. But for the life of him he couldn't remember where or when. She was certainly a pleasure to look at as she moved from tray to tray to pore over the blooms. Nothing size zero about this lady. She was delectably curvy in jeans and a plain white T-shirt, with a sweater knotted by its sleeves at her waist. The straight, heavy hair curving in below chin level was the exact sheen and colour of the conkers it would soon be his interminable job to help clear up, but the eyes she turned on him were dark, almond-shaped, and bright with that traffic-stopping smile again.

'There,' she said with satisfaction as he put the last tray on the trolley. 'Time to call a halt before I break the bank.'

'Our prices are very reasonable,' he assured her. 'Competitive, at least.'

'I'm sure they are. But we rather went mad today before I even started on the pansies. And now I must find my way back to the tribe. Thank you so much for your help.'

'My pleasure,' he assured her, and summoned a hovering assistant. 'Show the lady where to pay and take her back to the main entrance, please.'

'You've been a long time,' said her father, Jack Logan, when Jo rejoined the others. 'Madam here was getting restless.'

'Sorry. It was a really long way to the pansies.' She grinned. 'Funny thing, though, the way back was really short.'

Jack raised an eyebrow. 'Led up the garden path, were you?'

'Literally.' Her eyes danced. 'Which is flattering. My guide was very tasty under all that earth.'

'Tired,' wailed a small voice.

Her father smoothed the dark curls from the little face burrowed against his shoulder. 'All right, Kitty-cat, let's go home to Mummy. We've stowed the other plants in the car already, Jo. Are you staying on to look over the Hall?'

She hesitated, not sure she still felt like it, but then nodded. 'After making a fuss about driving myself here to do just that, I may as well. I'll leave my car here and walk over to see how the other half lives.'

'I could stay with you,' her grandfather offered, but she shook her head and kissed him lovingly.

'You look tired. Go home with Jack and Kitty, and tell Kate I did my best with the pansy selection. I'll ring later to see how she is.'

'I just hope she spent the afternoon in bed, as promised,' said Jack, frowning.

'If you'd stayed there with her she might have done,' said Jo. 'Grandpa and I could have brought Kitty to buy the plants.'

'The idea was to get Kate to rest.'

'So put Kitty to bed for her, then make a nice little supper for two.'

He smiled. 'That was my plan, Miss Bossy. Are you going to share it with us?'

'No. After my tour of the stately pile I'll drive straight home to my place and get an early night.' Jo reached up to kiss the drowsy child, then with a wave to her men set off along a carriageway that wound through undulating parkland for a longer distance than she'd expected before it reached the crenellated gatehouse of Arnborough Hall.

She bought a guidebook, handed over the substantial entrance fee, and then walked along a paved pathway through green velvet lawns to cross a moat so wide the ancient house appeared to float in it like an enchanted castle.

'I'm afraid you've missed the last tour of the day,' said a steward, when Jo entered the Great Hall. 'But if you care to look round on your own, please do. Your guidebook gives the route.'

'Thank you. I'll do my best not to trespass.' Jo gazed with pleasure at the lofty ceiling and the suits of armour in niches in the high stone walls. 'It's such an impressive space, yet the comfortable furniture gives it the feel of a huge, welcoming drawing room.'

The woman smiled. 'That's exactly what it is. On special occasions the family use it to entertain. Please take your time. Forty minutes yet before we close, and you'll find stewards everywhere to answer questions.'

'Thank you.' Jo was only too happy to explore alone. Guidebook at the ready, she started in the library to admire its wealth of books and a pair of magnificent terrestrial and celestial globes. The room smelt of old leather sweetened by potpourri, and she paused, frowning a little, sure she'd seen a room like this before. She had the same feeling in a small formal drawing room with gilded furniture, and again in a lofty dining room with a long table laid for a banquet. By the time she reached the ballroom she was convinced she'd visited Arnborough Hall in a former life, and indulged in a pleasant little fantasy—imagining herself twirling around in waltz-time under its magnificent chandeliers.

With no time to follow the usual visitors' route, she took a shortcut to a long gallery hung with her particular interest, the Hall's valuable paintings, which included, so the guidebook told her, a rare portrait by Constable. The family portraits dated from as far back as the early Tudor period, and Jo studied each one at length. She spotted a possible Holbein, and farther on a Stuart Lely, and in the Georgian section her eyebrows rose when she found both a Gainsborough and a Lawrence. But she slowed to a halt under the Victorian portraits. The resemblance between the men of the family in the nineteenth century was not only marked, there was something familiar about them. She'd seen the distinctive features of the Victorian Lord Arnborough and his sons before somewhere. In that other life again? Creepy. She sighed as she checked her watch. Time was up.

'I hope I haven't kept you waiting,' she apologised to the steward waiting to lock up in the Great Hall. 'I should have started earlier. I had to miss part of it.'

'Then do come again,' said the friendly woman. 'We have lots to offer in the run-up to Christmas, both here and at our garden centre.'

'Thank you. I will. Goodbye.'

As Jo left the gatehouse she felt a leap of pleasure as she spotted a tall figure in the distance. Her hot gardener looked very different now, in clean, elderly jeans and a white T-shirt which clung to his broad shoulders and lean waist. His shaggy ink-black hair was damp round the edges, and he was minus the dark stubble and sunglasses. As he came close, smiling in recognition, she drew in a deep, surreptitious breath. His eyes were the dark amber colour she associated with lions. Hot was right. He scrubbed up *really* well.

'Hello again,' he said warmly. 'You've been looking over the house?'

Jo nodded, smiling. 'The others went straight home from the

garden centre. I came under my own steam so I could look round the Hall afterwards.'

'Will your husband have your little girl in bed by the time you get home?'

'Actually that was my father, who looks far too young for the role, so I call him Jack. And Kitty's my little sister. If you want the complete picture, the handsome older gentleman in the family group was my grandfather.' To her delight a trace of colour showed along the knife-edge cheekbones.

'I do beg your pardon,' he said stiffly, then disarmed her with a grin. 'On the other hand, the no husband part is good news— or is there some other contender lurking around somewhere?'

Jo laughed and shook her head. 'No. I'm single.'

His eyes gleamed. 'Excellent—so am I! Let's celebrate our single blessedness with a drink before you drive home.'

Jo blinked. 'My word, you gardeners certainly don't beat about the bush!'

He shook his head. 'Life's too short for that. So will you come? The Arnborough Arms is just down the road. I'm March, by the way.' He held out a long brown hand.

She shook it formally. 'I'm Joanna, and I'm thirsty, so the answer's yes.'

'Right, then, Joanna. If we cross the gardens at this point we can take a shortcut along a footpath.'

'You obviously know the place well.'

'Man and boy. Are you expected for dinner with your family?'

She shook her head. 'I cooked lunch for them before we came, while Jack hovered around my mother—known to me as Kate, by the way—driving her mad by asking how she felt every few minutes.'

'She's under the weather?'

'Expecting another baby soon,' said Jo, sobering. 'Lord knows how my father will cope this time—he was bad enough when Kitty was born.' She pulled a face. 'Sorry! Too much information.'

'Not at all. You and your father have my sympathy.'

'Thank you.' She smiled up at him. 'By the way, I hope the pub boasts a comprehensive Ladies' room. I feel a bit grubby. And you've obviously been home for a bath since I saw you last.'

'Much needed,' he said with feeling. 'I'd been slaving away in the grafting house for hours.' He took her by the waist to swing her over the stile at the end of the overgrown footpath. 'Here we are: a couple of yards from the pub's back door. Hang on a minute—I'll have a word with the landlord.'

Jo watched as her new friend rapped at the closed door, then opened it to lean inside.

'It's not opening time yet?' she asked, when he came back to collect her.

'Open all day. I merely asked Dan if we could take over the back parlour to chat in peace. Otherwise you'll get trampled on by people playing darts and so on.'

The pub was attractive, with black beams and white plastered walls. It was also deserted. Jo raised an eyebrow at her escort as he ushered her into a small room behind the bar. 'Trampled on?'

'Sure to be later,' he said firmly. 'So, what's your fancy, Joanna?'

'Grapefruit juice with lemonade and lots of ice, please.'

Their drinks were waiting on a table in a window embrasure when she rejoined March after her repair session.

'I've been toiling all day, and I'm not driving, so I can indulge in a beer,' he said, and raised his glass to her. 'Your very good health, Joanna.'

'Do you live near by?'

'Just a short stroll, yes. How about you?'

'An hour's drive away.' She sipped gratefully. 'I was in need of that. Thank you.'

March leaned back, relaxed, his long legs stretched out. 'What did you think of the Hall?'

'It's a glorious place. I don't suppose the owner's single by any chance?' she said hopefully. 'If so I'll marry him and move in tomorrow.'

He laughed. 'You liked it that much?'

'It's the atmosphere. Ancient though it may be, it feels like a home.'

'Probably because the same family has lived there continuously from the fifteenth century.'

'Really?' She eyed him in awe. 'What an incredible feat.'

'Achieved because the succession swung from branch to branch a bit on the family tree, with the odd bridegroom taking on the bride's family name to keep things going. Did you take a look at the portraits in the Long Gallery?' he added casually.

'Not all of them. My time ran out halfway through Victoria's era.'

'Oh, bad luck,' he said, and sat back, relaxed. 'So tell me, Joanna, what do you do with your life?'

She sighed. 'You'll laugh.'

His eyes gleamed again. 'Why?'

'Other men do.'

March sat erect. 'I am not like other men,' he assured her with grandeur, then eyed her speculatively. 'Are you in entertainment of some kind?'

'Nothing so exciting. Shortly after I qualified my father's assistant left him to become a full time mother. He suggested I take over from her for a while until I decided what I wanted to do with my life. I liked the work from day one—still do—so there I am. Working for my father.'

'What does he do?'

'He's a builder.' Which was true enough. Up to a point.

'And you get on well together, obviously.'

'Professionally we make a really good team.' She smiled wryly. 'But my private life worries Jack. At times he gets all patriarchal and heavy about wanting me to live at home with him and Kate.'

His lips twitched. 'Why? Are you addicted to wild parties?'

'I wish!' She sobered. 'No, actually, I don't wish. I did that bit as a student. These days I lead a pretty ordinary life in my own little house near the park in town.'

March eyed her with respect. 'Your father must pay you well, then.' He threw up his hand like a fencer. 'Sorry. Rude. Forget I said that.'

'Actually, the house was a legacy. Where do you live?' she asked.

'In a sort of flat.'

Wondering what kind of money gardeners made—or didn't— Joanna changed the subject. 'Do you work every Sunday?'

'When I'm needed, yes. But not so much from now on. Then in December it gets hectic again.' He got up to collect her glass. 'Same again?'

'Yes, but it's my round!'

'I'll bring you the tab.' But when he came back with their glasses he handed her a menu. 'How about supper before you drive home? Or do you have something else on tonight?'

'No, not a thing.' She smiled warmly. 'Thank you. I'd like that. What's on offer?'

'Mainly salads on a Sunday evening. I can vouch for the ham. Trish, the landlord's wife, roasts it herself.'

Jo had eaten so little of the lunch she'd cooked for her family the prospect was suddenly very appealing. 'Then ham salad it is, please! But only if we go Dutch,' she added firmly.

She waited until March had strolled off to place their order, then to put her mind at rest rang Kate.

'Two Trish specials coming up,' March informed her as she put her phone away.

Jo smiled at him. 'I've just had a word with my mother, who feels better now, which means I can enjoy my meal. I was so worried about her at lunch that for once I didn't eat much.'

'Are you a good cook?'

'Yes.'

He laughed. 'No false modesty, then.'

She grinned. 'Not a shred. I've always liked cooking. I'm good at it. How about you?'

'I won't starve, but it's not my favourite pastime.'

'That's obviously gardening.'

To her surprise he shook his head. 'I merely follow orders from the tyrant who oversees the grounds at the Hall.'

'Is he elderly and curmudgeonly?'

'No. He's youngish and highly qualified—also the brain behind the garden centre.'

'So when he says jump you jump?'

'More or less. I've learnt a lot from him. Especially about roses.'

'I was told they're quite a feature here.'

March nodded. 'And not just in the gardens at the Hall. We sold a lot of them in bush form at the garden centre today, ready to put in for next year. You must come back in high summer, when the roses are at their glorious best. Though Ed underplants them with all manner of things to create colour and form in the beds all year round. He's an artist with colours. Did you look round outside?'

'I didn't have time.'

'Come back tomorrow and I'll beg an hour off to give you a tour.'

Jo grinned. 'Is that some kind of spin on showing me your etchings?'

He let out a snort of laughter. 'No. Though I do have an etching or two you could look at some time. But only when I know you *much* better.'

Jo chuckled, then looked up in anticipation as the landlord appeared with plates arranged and garnished with artistry. 'This looks wonderful!'

'Enjoy your meal,' said the man, pleased, and exchanged a

look with March. 'The place is filling up, so just give me the nod if you need anything.'

The salads were accompanied by a platter of rustic bread which looked so appetising Joanna's stomach growled. 'Oops—sorry!'

March grinned. 'Never mind the apologies—dig in. I'm starving.'

'This is delicious,' said Jo, tasting the ham. 'Do you eat here a lot?'

'Not as often as I'd like. But I indulge on a Sunday evening like this sometimes.'

'It must be good to have a meal put in front of you if you've been working all day!'

He nodded. 'Do you cook for yourself every night? Or do you have a succession of hopeful swains ready to wine and dine you?'

'Afraid not,' she said with regret. 'I have friends I eat out with on a fairly regular basis, but most nights I rustle up something in my little nest, or I yield to persuasion and eat with Kate and Jack. Sometimes my grandfather as well.'

'Does he live with your parents?'

'No. He won't budge from his own house. And, despite constant nagging from my father, I won't budge from mine, either '

'He'd like you under his eye at home?'

Jo nodded. 'Fortunately Kate refuses to support Jack on this. She appreciates my need for a place—and a life—of my own.'

March's lips twitched. 'While your father harbours dark thoughts about what you get up to in your little house!'

'Nothing tabloid-worthy,' she assured him. 'I just like having friends around—male or female—without his eagle eye on the proceedings. Would you fancy being watched all the time?'

'No,' he said, sobering, and eyed her empty plate in approval. 'You enjoyed that?'

'Absolutely—it was delicious. I'd quite like some coffee,

please, and then I must be on my way. Monday tomorrow, and Jack demands punctuality from his employees, whether related or not.'

Rather to Jo's surprise, March gathered up their plates himself and took them over to the bar when he ordered their coffee. As he eased into the seat again he leaned back at an angle to look into her face. 'I've enjoyed this enormously, Joanna. Let's do it again in some other location. Soon.'

She eyed him, taken aback. 'When?'

'I imagine tomorrow is probably rushing it a bit—how about Tuesday evening?'

She blinked. 'That soon?'

The intent leonine eyes held hers. 'After my session with you and the pansies I envied the man I took for granted was your husband,' he said, startling her. 'So when our paths crossed again I seized the day when I found you were unattached. As any man in his right mind would. So, then, Joanna—I'll see you on Tuesday.'

'Well—yes, all right,' she said warily.

'Excellent. Give me your telephone number and tell me how to get to your place. I'll pick you up at seven.' He glanced up. 'Dan's signalling. I'll just fetch our coffee. As you can hear, it's busy out there.'

When he got back March sat close enough for Jo to feel conscious, suddenly, of muscular tanned arms, and the scent of soap and warm man. Odd. None of this had registered before. But now March had made it clear this was to be no one-off occasion, she felt physically aware of him as the attractive male specimen he undoubtedly was.

'Doesn't anyone else use this parlour?' she asked.

'Not much on a Sunday.'

She eyed him militantly as she sipped her coffee. 'Right, then. How much was the bill?'

'Your turn to pay on Tuesday,' he said promptly.

'In that case don't expect Michelin stars!'

'The food is irrelevant,' he said dismissively. 'It's the company that matters.'

'I'll give it some thought.' She sighed as she glanced at her watch. 'I really must go.'

'I'll walk you to your car.'

'I'm afraid it's parked all the way back at the garden centre.'

'All to the good. Longer walk.'

She gave him a sidelong glance. 'Though not *much* longer than the trek you took me on to find the pansies!'

His eyes gleamed unrepentantly. 'I swear I don't make a practice of kidnapping married ladies. I persuaded myself that a few innocent minutes in your company hardly counted as adultery.'

Her lips twitched. 'Surely adultery has to be consensual?'

'No idea. That's one sin I've never committed.'

'Do tell about the others!'

'On Tuesday,' he promised.

Joanna sent her compliments to the chef when she said goodnight to the landlord. Outside in the starry darkness she shivered a little, and March helped her into her sweater, then took her hand as they walked down the quiet road leading to the garden centre.

'In case you stumble in uncharted territory,' he said lightly.

'Now we've left the pub behind it's so quiet here,' she commented, enjoying the contact.

'Too quiet sometimes. Occasionally I need a fix of city lights.'

She looked up at him. 'You live alone?'

'Yes, Joanna,' he said amused. 'As I told you, I'm single.'

'You could be living with your mother,' she suggested cheekily.

'She died some years ago; my father more recently.'

'I'm so sorry.' Joanna squeezed his hand, full of sympathy for anyone who lacked parents. 'Thank you for the meal, March. I enjoyed it—and the evening—very much.'

He smiled down at her as they reached her car. 'So did I. A pity you have to go home so early.' He bent and kissed her cheek. 'I'll pick you up at seven on Tuesday.'

In her car mirror Jo could see March standing under the overhead light, watching her out of sight. She drove home in a thoughtful mood. It was useless to pretend she hadn't been delighted with everything about the entire evening, including March's demand to repeat it so soon. The unruly hair and easy laid-back manner—and those eyes—appealed to her strongly. He'd been so easy to talk to she'd been more forthcoming about herself than usual. Nevertheless, she had an idea that a very strong personality lay behind the effortless charm. No Jekyll and Hyde stuff—just a feeling that there was far more to him than met the eye—like a surname, she thought suddenly. Or maybe March *was* his surname. She'd forgotten to ask.

CHAPTER TWO

WHEN she turned into Park Crescent later, Jo felt her usual rush of pleasure as she drew up outside her house. As simple as a child's drawing, its white walls glimmered under the street lamp, and a welcome shone through the fanlight over the blue door, due to her father's insistence on security lights. Until she'd been old enough to live here alone the house had been let out to tenants, but the moment the final lease had terminated Tom Logan had begun redecorating the entire house for his adored granddaughter, delighted that she'd chosen to revert to the original paint colours she'd helped choose for it in her teens.

When her phone rang the moment she got in Jo was surprised—and delighted—to find her caller was March.

'Good,' he said. 'You're home.'

'Just this minute. Thank you again for supper.'

'A small return for your company, Joanna. Now I know you're safe and sound I'll let you get that early night. Until Tuesday, then. Goodnight.'

'Goodnight—wait.' But he'd rung off. So he was still plain March.

Jo thought long and hard about her hot gardener while she got ready for bed. He was obviously well educated, with the speech patterns and the air of bred-in-the-bone assurance common to the old Etonians she'd met in college. March had obviously been schooled if not at Eton, at some similar place of learning. But it was equally obvious that he was down on his luck these days. Jo frowned, wishing now that she'd insisted on paying her share of the meal. She might work for her father, but like all his employees she was well paid. So to avoid any hurt male pride on Tuesday she would treat March to some home cooking.

Feeding hungry male visitors was nothing unusual. Leo and Josh Carey, the twins who were her oldest and closest male friends, were both trainee doctors, and they worked such punishing hours at the local hospital they were only too glad to collapse at Jo's kitchen table during an hour or two off and devour, either separately or together, whatever food she put in front of them.

'Nice evening?' said her father, when Jo arrived at Logan Development next morning.

'Very pleasant. How's Kate today?' she added anxiously.

Jack heaved a sigh. 'Tired. The baby's not giving her much rest at night.'

'You either, by the look of you,' she said with concern. 'How about some coffee?'

He patted her hand. 'What would I do without you?'

'Make your own coffee?'

He chuckled. 'So, tell me about this gardener.'

She gave him a Cheshire Cat smile. 'He's a charmer. I like him.'

'Charm,' said her father darkly, 'is not the most important qualification on a man's CV. Are you seeing him again?'

'Yes. Tomorrow night.'

His eyebrows rose. 'Are you, indeed? Does your mother know?'

'Not yet. I'll ring Kate later. Don't worry, I'm a big girl now, boss.' Jo smiled at him as she handed him a steaming cup, then made for her own office. 'Time to get my nose to the grindstone.'

Jack Logan gazed after her as he drank the coffee, still, after all these years, amazed by his luck with the women in his life. He frowned, wishing he'd paid more attention to the gardener who'd taken so long to show Joanna the pansies. He'd never considered himself a violent man, but he knew from experience that he was ready to inflict grievous bodily harm on any man that caused his daughter the slightest grief. And soon there would be another little Logan in the mix. Jack shivered and picked up the phone, wishing that the love of his life was safely through the birth.

'Kate? Are you feeling better now, my darling?'

Although she knew she looked good in the mannish white shirt and black velvet jeans, Jo felt surprisingly nervous as she waited for her dinner guest to arrive. The table in the small dining room was laid with her best china, plus silverware borrowed for the occasion. The wine was breathing, the Beef Wellington was ready and would rest happily until March arrived—if he was punctual. She grinned suddenly. Josh and Leo would tease her unmercifully if they saw her fussing like this. She'd cooked countless meals for them, and for her family, without turning a hair. But this was different. She was so deep in thought she jumped yards when the doorbell rang. She threw her apron on a chair, took in a deep breath, and went to open the door.

March stood smiling down at her. His tanned face looked even darker against a white shirt, and his suit was the casual, unstructured kind that could have been either charity shop or Armani. But it was nevertheless a suit.

'Hi,' she said, wishing she'd worn a dress.

'Hi, yourself. What a delightful house, Joanna!'

'Thank you. Come in.' She led him into the parlour and waved him to the sofa. 'What can I get you to drink?'

He eyed the small room with such admiration Jo's heart warmed to him. 'I'd better have something soft if we're driving any distance. I wasn't sure what you had in mind, but I put a tie in my pocket in case it's somewhere formal.'

'It's not,' she informed him. 'Having boasted about my cooking, I decided to let you judge it for yourself.'

His eyes lit up with the familiar gleam. 'We're eating here?'

She nodded. 'So, how about a beer? Or would you like a glass of the red wine breathing in the kitchen?'

'Perfect.'

'Good. Make yourself comfortable and I'll fetch it.'

'I'll come with you and fetch it myself.'

'There's not much room,' she warned.

March followed her down the hall to her kitchen, recently refitted with plain white cupboards and a Belfast sink. Due to a frantic tidying session before her guest arrived the only notes of colour came from a potted cyclamen, a bowl of fruit, and the heap of prepared vegetables waiting for the pot.

'Small, but perfect. And something smells wonderful,' he added, sniffing the air.

Jo smiled, pleased, and handed him a glass of wine. 'There are some nuts and so on in the parlour. If you go back in I'll deal with the vegetables. I'll be with you in a minute.'

'I'd rather stay here and watch.' He leaned against the counter, looming large in the small space.

'As you like.' Long accustomed to an audience as she cooked, Jo wasn't flustered by the eyes watching her so closely. Not much. 'Right,' she said at last, putting the lid on the steamer. 'Just twenty minutes or so for the vegetables and we'll be there. No first course, I'm afraid. Will you take my glass of wine too, please?' She set a timer and took it with her as they went back to the parlour.

Her guest eyed her with respect as he handed her wine over. 'If you carry out your job as efficiently as you cook, your father's a lucky man.'

Jo smiled. 'You haven't tasted the food yet,' she warned.

'If it tastes half as good as it smells I'll be happy,' he assured her, and raised his glass in toast. 'This is such a pleasure, Joanna.'

'Have you been stuck inside all day again today?' she asked.

'No. I went on an in-depth tour of the gardens and grounds at the Hall, listening with attention as the tyrant in charge outlined his plans for next year.'

'Did you contribute any ideas?'

'Several. Who knows? Ed may even use some of them.'

Jo laughed. 'He's obviously very full of himself, this horticultural genius.'

March shook his head. 'Genius, yes, but Ed's not full of himself at all. He just loves his work. So, what have you done today?' he added.

'I've been chasing up suppliers and contractors.' She pulled a face. 'Much smoothing over was necessary. The boss was a bit abrasive yesterday.'

'And you won them over?'

'Of course—you catch more flies with honey!' She jumped up as her alarm went off. 'Time to put dinner together.'

He got up quickly. 'I'll come with you.'

Joanna shook her head. 'At this stage I work better alone. Why don't you read the paper for five minutes until I call?'

March opened the door for her. 'I'd be only too happy to help.'

'I may take you up on that later.'

Left alone, March took a look round the room, hoping to learn more about Joanna from her taste in literature. An alcove alongside the fireplace held an eclectic mix of classics, large illustrated books on fine art, and rows of paperback bestsellers with the accent on gruesome crime. No romantic fiction. He pulled out a dog-eared anthology of poems, and grinned as he saw the flyleaf. Joanna Sutton, Form 3A. He put it back and moved on to the watercolour studies grouped on two of her walls. He nodded, impressed. The subtle tints were exactly right for the understated charm of the room.

March turned as the door opened. 'I was just admiring your artwork.'

Joanna smiled. 'Good, aren't they? All local scenes. A talented friend of mine painted them. Right, then, come with me—dinner is served.'

In the small dining room candles flickered in crystal holders to highlight the central platter of colourful vegetables surrounding a golden-crusted Beef Wellington.

'What a wonderful sight,' said March in awe.

'Do sit down.' Jo filled their glasses, then took up a carving knife. 'I should have done this in the kitchen, but I wanted you to see my creation in all its glory first.'

'Glory is the right word,' he agreed, as she served him a substantial slice of rare beef encased in perfect crisp pastry.

'Help yourself to the rest,' said Joanna. She served herself, then sat down and held up her glass. 'Happy eating.'

March raised his own. 'To the beautiful chef.'

They fell on the food with equal enthusiasm. 'I enjoy my own cooking,' she admitted. 'My artist friend, Isobel James, cooks great meals. But, unlike me, by the time she gets them to the table she can never eat much herself.'

'This is superb,' said March indistinctly. 'It would be tragedy if you couldn't eat it. What's the bit between the meat and pastry?'

'Duxelle of mushrooms. Nice, isn't it?'

'Nice? It's glorious!'

'Have some more.' Joanna got up to serve him.

'Who taught you to cook like this?' March asked. 'Your mother?'

Joanna shook her head. 'I learned this kind of thing from Molly Carter, who used to be Jack's cook and housekeeper before he married Kate. Molly owns a restaurant in town these days.'

'I'll take you there next time, then,' said March promptly, and grinned at the look on her face. 'Or am I breaking the speed barrier again?'

'Not exactly.' She smiled. 'But let's enjoy this evening before we move on to the next.'

'Enjoy is the word.' He applied himself to the rest of his dinner. 'Tell me more about yourself, Joanna. I noticed several books on art on your shelves.'

'I did Fine Art in college for a while.'

'Where?'

'Oxford.' She put down her knife and fork and drank some wine.

'Weren't you happy there?'

Her face shadowed. 'In the beginning I loved it, but it didn't work out for me. So at the end of the first year I left the dreaming spires and came back here to take a business course at the local technical college.'

March eyed her with respect. 'That must have been a big adjustment after Fine Art at Oxford.'

'It certainly was.'

'It must have helped to have this house to get back to?'

She shook her head. 'I had to wait for the tenant's lease to expire before I could move in.'

'You lived with your parents until then?'

'For almost a year.' She smiled at him wryly, her eyes bright in the flickering candlelight. 'I'd been away at school since I was eight, and went straight from there to Oxford. No gap year for me. So, much as I love my parents, it was quite an adjustment to live permanently at home in Mill House.' Hey, watch it, she warned herself, and collected the plates to change the subject. The man was so easy to talk to she'd be telling him all her secrets if she wasn't careful. Not her usual policy with someone she knew so little. Or even with people she knew well. She smiled brightly. 'I didn't have time to make a pudding, but I can give you cheese with home-made biscuits—another of Molly's recipes.'

March got up, curious about the shutter she'd suddenly

pulled down between them. Ignoring her protests, he picked up the heavy platter to follow her into the kitchen.

He was obviously someone used to doing things for himself, noted Jo, and it was making her more and more curious about him. 'Just leave it on the counter,' she told him. 'I don't put this in the dishwasher.'

'I'm good at washing up. Let's do it now.'

She shook her head. 'If there's a next time, you can do it then.'

'Next time,' he said, moving closer, 'I'll take you out to dinner. But,' he added deliberately, 'I'll insist on washing up the time after that. Shall I take the cheese in?'

'Thank you. I'll make some coffee.' Glad to be alone for a moment, Jo frowned while the coffee-maker did its thing. She liked this relaxed, self-assured man very much, but the way he took so much for granted was a bit unnerving. She smiled wryly. On the other hand it was only human to feel gratified when a man of March's calibre made it so plain he was interested in her.

'I couldn't resist trying your biscuits,' he confessed when she rejoined him. 'You're a very talented cook, Joanna. Have you ever thought of it as a career?'

She pulled a face. 'Lord, no. When I came back here after—after Oxford, I worked for Molly that summer, then did weekends and holiday periods for her when I started the new course. So I know what fiendishly hard work it is. I enjoy a little social entertaining now and then, but that's as far as it goes.'

'Who do you entertain?'

'Josh and Leo Carey mostly—twin brothers I've known for years. And I don't exactly entertain them—just feed them whenever they've got an hour off. Then there's Isobel, the artist whose work you liked. We met at a party when we were thirteen, and we've been firm friends ever since. She lives in an attic flat above the art gallery she manages in town.'

March looked at her steadily. 'But no boyfriend for you, Joanna?'

She raised an eyebrow. 'If there were you wouldn't be here tonight.'

'Point taken. But you're a pleasure to look at, gainfully employed, you own a jewel of a house—and you cook like an angel.' He spread his hands. 'Why hasn't some man snapped you up long since?'

Joanna kept her eyes on the coffee she was pouring. 'Because I don't want to be snapped up.'

'Is that written in stone?' He took the cup she handed him. 'Because be warned, Joanna. I intend to know you better. Much better.'

'Are you suggesting we become lovers?' she said bluntly.

March drained his cup and set it down with a click. 'No, I'm not.'

'I had to ask.'

'Well, now you have. And, since we're calling a spade a spade here, I won't pretend the thought hadn't crossed my mind.' His eyes speared hers. 'But that's not my reason for being here tonight. I came to enjoy your company, so relax. I don't have any shortcuts to paradise in mind right now. These twins you mentioned,' he added. 'Since they eat here regularly, I take it neither of them aspires to a closer relationship with you?'

Joanna shook her head, kicking herself for bringing the subject up. 'They're like brothers. I'm very fond of them, but they irritate me sometimes, too.'

'Because they're men?'

'Right.' She smiled crookedly. 'The only man I know who never irritates me is my grandfather.'

'Not your father?'

'Jack's too dictatorial not to irritate me sometimes, but I love him just the same.'

'Fortunate man.' March raised a quizzical eyebrow. 'So, Joanna, where do we stand, you and I?'

She thought it over. 'I'd like us to be friends,' she said cautiously.

'Then we will be. Your house is a surprise,' he added, stretching out his long legs.

'In what way?'

'Because you look like modern woman personified I expected contemporary furnishings and abstract art.'

Jo chuckled. 'Anachronism in a nineteenth century house, March. Besides,' she added, 'this is how the house was when it was made over to me. I helped Kate choose the paint colours and some of the furnishings eleven years ago. When I was thirteen,' she said demurely, 'in case you're wondering. But the chairs and some of the other pieces in the house belonged to the aunt who left it to Kate. How about you?' she added. 'Is your place all minimalist and leather?'

'God, no—anything but!' March's eyes fastened on hers. 'So. Now it's established that my intentions are honourable, when can I see you again?'

'Next week?'

March jumped up and pulled her to her feet and into his arms. 'This weekend,' he said firmly, and planted a kiss on her lips. He raised his head to look into her eyes, then kissed her again. 'Saturday. Make a reservation for two at your friend Molly's.'

Jo nodded rather than trust her voice.

He smiled triumphantly. 'Good. I'll ring you to find out the details. And now I'd better leave—before you change your mind.'

'I won't. How about some more coffee before you go?' she suggested, surprised by how much she wanted him to stay a while.

'Wonderful idea,' he said, as he opened the door for her, giving thanks that he hadn't frightened her off by kissing her. It had been a risk worth taking.

To Jo's relief March did not follow her to the kitchen, which gave her time to recover from the kisses which, though brief, she could still feel like a brand on her mouth. He turned with a smile as she returned to the parlour with two mugs of coffee.

'Your taste in literature is unexpected, Joanna.'

'Ah, but I keep the cookbooks in the kitchen, and my romances and Georgette Heyers lurk upstairs in my little study! I enjoy a happy ending as much as any other female.'

'I'm delighted to hear it.' He took one of the mugs, impressed to find his coffee was black with a touch of sugar. 'Perfect. You're a very efficient hostess.'

'Molly says the details are important, so I try to remember the various tastes of my guests. Not,' Jo added wryly, 'that it matters with the Carey twins. They eat whatever I put in front of them.'

March returned to the sofa. 'You've known them a long time?'

'Ten years or so. I met them at a very sad time in my young life, and they were a huge help.'

'What happened?'

She looked at him for a moment. 'Like your etchings, that's best left until I know you better.'

'Which,' he informed her very deliberately, 'you will do. And sooner rather than later—Miss Sutton.' He grinned at her startled look. 'I investigated your taste in poetry just now. Your name was on the flyleaf.'

'I see,' she said slowly. 'Which reminds me: I still don't know *your* other name.'

He drained his coffee mug and stood up. 'It's Aubrey. And now I really must go. I have a lot to do tomorrow.'

'Back in the grafting house again?'

'No. The weather forecast is good for the next week, which means I'm on grass-cutting detail while the weather holds.'

Jo stared at him in awe. 'It's your job to cut all that grass?'

'Afraid so.' He grinned. 'Did you imagine I got this tan in Barbados?'

She eyed him in sudden doubt. 'Look, we don't have to go

to Molly's on Saturday. There are other places to eat—I could even drive to your local again.'

'Absolutely not. It's too far for you at that time of night.' He moved closer. 'Joanna, I swear I can spring for dinner for two with no problem—even at your friend Molly's establishment.'

She flushed. 'I didn't mean to offend you, March.'

'But you did,' he said promptly. 'You wounded my male pride. So kiss it better, please.' He took her in his arms and tipped her face up to his. 'Just a nice, friendly kiss between friends to say you're sorry.' But when their lips met the kiss heated to a long way short of mere friendly before he finally released her.

'Thank you again, Joanna,' he said, in tones very different from his usual lazy drawl. 'Goodnight.'

'Goodnight,' she said breathlessly. 'Drive safely.'

CHAPTER THREE

JOANNA cleared away in thoughtful mood. So he was March Aubrey. While he thought she was Joanna Sutton. Which she had been—at one time. But to explain would mean taking March into confidences about her adoptive parents. Far too personal with someone she'd known such a short time. Perhaps she should go back to Arnborough Hall Nurseries and make a few discreet enquiries before she got too involved. Because involved she was likely to be if she went on seeing March Aubrey on a regular basis. She hadn't been kissed like that in a long time. Or ever.

Jo gave a sigh of relief later as she slid into the beautiful sleigh bed which had been part of Kate's legacy from her aunt who, though single all her life, had probably not, according to Kate, been a maiden aunt. Definitely not, thought Jo, stretching. A bed like this was made for lovers. Which was why she made sure no male guest ever laid eyes on it. But the sudden thought of sharing the bed with March Aubrey was so unsettling she arrived at Logan Development next morning with shadows under her eyes.

'The gardener kept you out late last night?' said her father affably.

'No,' she said with truth.

'Did you have a good meal?'

'Yes.' Also truthful. 'How's Kate this morning?'

Jack's eyes, rimmed with darker marks of fatigue than hers, met hers unhappily. 'She's very tired. A man feels so bloody helpless at times like this—not to mention guilty. Which,' he added hastily, 'is hardly something to discuss with my daughter.'

'Jack,' she said gently. 'Stop worrying. Loads of women have babies in their forties these days.'

'I know, but because it's *my* woman it doesn't help.' He heaved a sigh. 'All right. Let's get to work. What's first up in the diary?'

The diary was full and the day was hectic. Jo was glad. It helped keep her mind off March. But only temporarily. When she got home a van marked with the logo of Arnborough Hall Nurseries was parked near her house. A young man emerged from it, eyeing her hopefully as he held out a giant sheaf of flowers.

'Miss Joanna Sutton?'

'Yes.' More or less.

'These are for you.'

'How lovely. Thank you.' Jo let herself into the house as the van drove away, eager to read the card tucked into the blooms.

With my thanks. Until Saturday. March.

As if she needed reminding. Jo eyed the extravagant bouquet in disapproval, hoping March had been given a discount at the nurseries for something so pricey. It was also a long way for delivery, which added to the expense. She must make it plain on Saturday that extravagant gestures like this were unnecessary. A text to say thank you for the meal would have done. Jo arranged the flowers in a tall ceramic pot, set the spectacular result on the floor under the parlour window, and then sent a text of thanks to March, before hurrying upstairs to exchange her office suit for jeans and sweatshirt. After that it was straight back out to drive to Mill House and play with Kitty, then take over bathtime duty while their parents enjoyed a peaceful pre-dinner drink together.

'Mummy's going to buy a baby soon,' announced Kitty, when Jo was helping her into her pyjamas.

Oh, boy. As far as Jo knew the subject hadn't been mentioned to Kitty before. 'How wonderful,' she said brightly, lifting her onto her lap. 'You'll like having a baby brother or sister.'

'Mmm.' Kitty sighed as she snuggled close. 'But I can't choose.'

'It doesn't matter,' said Jo carefully, smoothing the dark curls. 'Either one will be lovely.'

'That's what Daddy said. Will you read me a story?'

'Of course I will. The one about the little bear?'

'I wish I'd gone with you on Sunday,' said Kate later, over supper. 'But it's such a trek to Arnborough. I've never been to the new garden centre there—nor, oddly enough, to the Hall itself. Is it worth a visit, Jo?'

'Definitely. Fabulous old house, dreamy gardens—you'd love it. I'm going back myself some time, to see the bits I missed. I got there too late to see everything.'

'Because she took so long to choose your pansies,' Jack told his wife. 'We were about to send out a search party by the time she got back.'

'I wasn't that long,' protested Jo, laughing. 'And you must admit they were first-class plants, Kate. They look fabulous in those stone troughs.'

'Don't they just! Grandpa put them in for me.' Kate shot a look at her daughter. 'So, are you seeing this gardener of yours again?'

'Yes. Saturday. I've made a reservation at Molly's.'

'So Molly gets to meet him before we do,' commented Jack. 'You'd better bring him here some time, too, so we can look him over.'

'No,' said Jo flatly.

'Why not?' asked Kate mildly. 'Are you ashamed of us?'

'No, of course not.' Jo got up to collect plates. 'You're just not up to it right now, Kate. Besides, if he comes here and sees this place, and the penny drops about Logan Development and so on, it could embarrass him.'

'Or,' said Jack with edge, 'he might think he's landed in the honey pot.'

Jo glared at him. 'Always a possibility. Either way, I won't be inviting him home to meet the family any time soon. Thanks just the same.'

Jo couldn't get her father's words out of her head when she was in bed that night. March, who lived in a 'sort of flat', had been impressed enough by her place. Heaven knew how he'd react to huge, spacious Mill House, which Jack had restored so magnificently that articles on it featured in magazines. Jo sighed. She wanted March to like her for herself, not for any expectations he might think she had. She'd been down that road before. She tossed and turned restlessly as she remembered how quick he'd been to veto a return visit to the Arnborough Arms. He obviously didn't want her back on his home ground, either.

It was a trying week. Jack's honey pot syndrome occupied her so much that at one stage Jo even considered ringing March to cancel. But then she'd have to explain why. To her surprise— and mounting disappointment—she heard nothing from March all week. When he finally rang her on the Friday evening she tensed, sure he was about to pre-empt her and do the cancelling himself.

'How are you, Joanna?' he asked.

'A bit weary. End of the week and all that. How about you?'

'Very tired of grass. Aren't you going to congratulate me?'

'On what?'

'For waiting until now to ring you. Are you impressed by my restraint?'

'Yes,' she said, laughing, suddenly so happy to hear that deep, drawling voice she didn't care why he liked her as long as he did. 'Deeply impressed.'

'Did you miss me?'

'Yes.'

There was silence for a moment. 'I wonder,' he said slowly, 'if you realise how that makes me feel.'

'Pleased, I hope.'

'Massive understatement.'

'That's nice. I booked with Molly by the way,' she added. 'Seven-thirty for eight.'

'Good. I'll be with you at seven.'

'Do you have more grass to cut before you come?'

'No, thank God. Hand weeding tomorrow.'

'No day off after all that grass?'

'Not a chance. Nor do I want one. The time would drag too much until I see you again. What will you do with your Saturday morning?'

'Kate has insisted that Jack play a round of golf with Grandpa tomorrow, to de-stress, so to make sure he does that I'll keep her company and play with Kitty—who now knows about the baby. I think she hankers after a little sister.'

He chuckled. 'How about you?'

'I just want a healthy baby and my mother in good shape.'

'Amen to that! Goodnight, Joanna.'

'Goodnight, March.'

Next day Jo played with Kitty for most of the morning, as planned, then ate the sandwich lunch Kate made for them. When Jack and her grandfather arrived, Jo put up with more teasing about her date, then drove off to do some food shopping, and took a detour on the way home to have a word with Molly.

The restaurant was ideally situated, halfway along a side-street of exclusive shops, with a solitary initial '*M*' in gold on the glass door. Having timed her visit until well after the lunch-time rush, Jo smiled at the handsome man who came hurrying to greet her.

'Molly in the back?'

'As always.' Angelo kissed her on both cheeks. 'You are very beautiful today, Joanna.'

'Thank you, Angelo. So are you.'

He grinned and kissed his fingers to her as she went through to the spotless kitchen, where Molly Carter was directing her minions through preparations for the evening's menu like a general readying troops for battle. She looked up with a broad smile.

'Hi! So who are you bringing here tonight, then, love? Is it a celebration? Don't tell me you're marrying one of the twins!'

Jo shook her head, grinning. 'I'd have to marry both of them, and I don't think that's allowed. It's not a celebration tonight. Just dinner for two.'

'I know that!' said Molly impatiently. 'But is your date a man?'

'Yes.'

'Good. Do I know him?'

'I shouldn't think so. I don't know him that well myself.'

Molly checked the stock one of her crew was making, then looked up at Jo, her eyes narrowed. 'Nice?'

'Very. So I want something special. What have you got?'

'All my food is special,' retorted Molly. 'But the sea bass is exceptional, and the saddle of lamb had such a good slug of gin in the marinade the meat will melt in the mouth.' She frowned. 'Why don't you cook a meal for him yourself? Lord knows I taught you well enough.'

'I did that last week. Beef Wellington.'

'Showy, but reliable. Did he like it?'

'He certainly ate a lot of it.' Jo hesitated. 'The thing is, Moll, he thinks my name is Sutton, and for now I want him to keep thinking that. So has Angelo booked me down as Logan?'

Molly eyed her quizzically. 'What are you playing at, my girl?'

'I'd just rather my date didn't know I was Jack's daughter—for a while, anyway.'

'Ah! You want to be loved for yourself, not Daddy's cash. All right. I'll brief Angelo and ask him to reserve one of the parking spaces outside. Now, tell me, how's Kate?'

By the time the doorbell rang that evening, prompt to the minute at seven, Jo had changed her dress once, her earrings twice, and persuaded herself that she would be happy in the red-soled black shoes which added five inches to her height and a touch of glamour to last year's little black dress. She took in a deep breath, then opened it to smile at March, who was even browner of face than before, but with hair newly trimmed, and impressive in a formal dark suit.

'Good evening, Miss Sutton.' He gave her a comprehensive look from head to toe and bent to kiss her on both cheeks. 'You look delectable.'

'Thank you,' she said, and closed the door. 'I really must thank you again for the flowers. They were very extravagant, but I won't scold you this time.'

He frowned as he followed her into the parlour. 'You don't like flowers?'

'Of course I do, but you shouldn't have gone to such expense. A text to say thank you would have been quite enough.'

He looked down his nose at her with hauteur, which was not, she saw with dismay, meant as a joke. 'Enough for you, possibly, but not for me. I was simply expressing my appreciation.'

'Oh, dear, I've offended you again.'

'Yes.' He moved closer, the hauteur heating to a predatory gleam. 'So what are you going to do about it?'

She backed away. 'If I kiss you better I'll ruin all my hard work!'

'Which would be a shame.' He ran a finger down her cheek. 'Apply the necessary balm later. When I bring you home.'

'I'll consider it. Would you like a drink?'

He shook his head. 'I'll save myself for a glass of wine over dinner. Does your friend Molly keep a good cellar?'

'Her front-of-house man sees to that side of the business. The restaurant has quite a name for its wine list.'

'Then, if my lady is ready, shall we?' March smiled at her, and Jo smiled back, amazed, now, that she had even thought of cancelling their evening.

Outside, March handed Jo into an E-type Jaguar so far from its first youth it was almost a museum piece.

'You've had this a long time?' she commented as they headed for town.

'Since I was old enough to drive.' He patted the steering wheel. 'Temperamental sometimes, but I love her just the same. Now, give me directions, please.'

March was impressed when he saw the reserved sign in a parking place right outside the restaurant.

'So you'll be able to keep an eye on her all evening,' teased Jo as March helped her out.

'Certainly not. I shall be keeping my eye—both eyes—on you,' he assured her as they entered to a warm welcome from Angelo.

'Joanna, *cara*!' He gave her his usual double kiss.

'Hi, Angelo, this is March Aubrey.'

'Good to meet you,' said March, holding out his hand.

'*Piacere*,' said Angelo, shaking it enthusiastically. 'Welcome.' He led them to one of the twin bay windows, and seated Joanna with a flourish at the last unoccupied table in the buzzing restaurant.

'I shall send someone to give you menus, but do not order drinks. Champagne waits ready chilled for you. On the house, with Molly's compliments,' he added.

'How lovely—do thank her for us,' said Joanna.

'VIP treatment,' commented March, impressed, as Angelo went off to summon a waiter.

'Partly because I used to work here,' Jo informed him. 'And partly to impress the first-time customer who's paying tonight.'

'Is that still worrying you, Joanna?'

'No. So stop looking down your nose at me.'

He grinned and sat back as a waitress put a carafe of water on the table, slid menus in front of them and then gave way to a waiter bearing champagne in an ice bucket. March looked on with approval as the man held the cork and twisted the bottle, and achieved a perfect wisp of smoke instead of a loud pop.

'What do you recommend, Joanna?' asked March, when they were left to study the menus.

'I've never eaten any meal here that was less than delicious,' she told him, fervently hoping that tonight would be no exception.

Eventually they both chose crab soufflé tarts to start, followed by the gin-tenderised lamb, and as they sat back to enjoy their champagne Angelo appeared with an *amuse bouche*—a liqueur glass of iced tomato consommé.

'Enjoy your meal,' he said, and retreated to his post to keep an expert eye on the crowded room.

'That packed quite a punch,' remarked March, eying the empty glass with respect. 'A hint of vodka?'

Jo nodded. 'And a pinch of cayenne—maybe even chilli.'

'Augurs well for the rest of the meal.' March raised his champagne glass in toast. 'What shall we drink to?'

'Friendship,' she said firmly.

He smiled and touched his glass to hers. '*Close* friendship.'

To Jo's relief the meal was everything she had hoped for. When Molly joined them at the end of it, bearing *petit fours* to accompany their coffee, March rose to thank her for the champagne, and said, with complete sincerity, that the only meal he'd enjoyed as much in recent memory had been Joanna's Beef Wellington.

'Why, thank you,' said Molly, her face flushed with pleasure. 'I taught her well, didn't I?'

Molly stayed chatting for a while, then left to talk with the other diners on her way back to her domain.

'You see now why I refused pudding,' said Joanna, eyeing the selection of *petits fours*.

'She's quite a surprise,' said March, watching Molly's progress.

'Because she's small and blonde?'

'No, because she's so young.'

'Molly must be thirty-three or so now. But she's always had tunnel vision about owning her own restaurant.' Joanna smiled. 'Her success was never in doubt, according to Jack.'

'He was right. Is a full house the norm here for a Saturday night?'

'It's the norm most nights—and Christmas is frantic. Molly does a sideline in seasonal corporate parties and so on, but she would never let me help out at those.' Jo pulled a face. 'She kept me firmly in the kitchen, so I refined my cooking skills instead of getting my bottom pinched. Though things rarely get out of hand. Molly's a terror if anyone hits on one of her girls—or boys, if it comes to that.'

March smiled. 'And what role does Angelo play?'

'Peace-keeper. He's the arch-soother of ruffled feathers— including hers. And don't be fooled by the movie star looks. He's got a great head for business, plus an encyclopaedic knowledge of wine. He's also her partner in private.'

'And that works?'

'Like a charm. Even Molly admits he's the one person who can handle her.'

March glanced over to the bar, where Angelo was laughing with some departing customers. 'You're right about the looks.'

'He's also really loving and funny. They suit each other.' Jo smiled at him. 'Shall we have more coffee at home?'

March rose with alacrity. 'I'll just settle up.'

As she chatted to Angelo, Jo couldn't help noticing that March paid the not inconsiderable amount, including a sizeable tip for the staff, in cash, instead of the usual credit card. Not that she would spoil things by mentioning it.

On the way home she couldn't help wondering if he meant to seize her the moment they were through her door, demanding balm for the wound she'd dealt to his pride earlier. But March merely took her key to unlock her door, then followed her to the kitchen to watch while she made coffee.

'That was a superb meal,' he commented. 'Your friend Molly's right up there with the best in chef terms. And yet you say she worked for your father before she struck out on her own?'

'Yes. Jack took her on straight out of catering college. She says she honed her skills on him.'

March hefted the tray to follow her to the parlour, but before he could start doing sums about Molly and her father Jo preempted him with a question of her own.

'Do you have any siblings, March?'

He took the coffee she offered him and sat down. 'One sister a couple of years my junior, married to a film producer, and a brother several years younger,' he added, sobering.

'Is he a gardener, too?'

'No.'

Jo waited, but when he said nothing more she drank her coffee in silence, trying not to feel offended.

'He was in a car accident when he was in college,' said March at last.

'Was he badly hurt?'

'Severe concussion, broken jaw and a mangled leg. The driver got off with a few cuts and bruises, loss of licence and a charge of dangerous driving. He was lucky to get away with a heavy fine instead of a custodial sentence.'

Jo eyed him with compassion. 'That must have been terrible for you.'

'I don't want another phone call like the one I received that night,' he agreed fervently. 'When my father and I got to the hospital my brother was delirious, muttering wildly about some friend through the metal clamp holding his jaw together. The driver had been sedated, so I couldn't check with him, but the police assured me that no one else had been in the car. By the time he was better Rufus had no recall of the accident at all, so I didn't bring the subject up again.'

'What happened afterwards?' asked Jo, her heart thumping.

'Rufus had been doing a Fine Art course, so the neurologist encouraged him to paint as therapy. It worked. When he was well enough my sister took him off to Italy to convalesce, and Rufus decided to resume his studies there instead of returning to Oxford. He's very talented. But for him that entire night, the events that led up to it, and most of his stay in hospital still remain a complete blank.' March thrust a hand through his hair, frowning as he saw the look on her face. 'I'm sorry, Joanna. I didn't mean to put a damper on our evening.'

'Did you search for this friend you mentioned? Do you think he was to blame?'

'No. I simply thought if I could set Rufus' mind at rest about the friend it would help him recover.'

She braced herself. 'What was the name he kept repeating?'

'Joe Logan.'

Although she'd known, deep down, what his answer would be, the words struck her like a blow to the heart.

March eyed her with concern. 'What's wrong?'

'I'm afraid that's me.' She met his eyes bravely. 'I'm Jo Logan.'

'*What*?' March stared blankly.

'I'm Jo Logan,' she repeated unhappily.

'You said your name was Sutton!'

'No, I didn't. You saw that in my school book. Sutton was the name of my adoptive parents. When I was thirteen they died, and I came to live with Kate. When she married Jack Logan I took his name.'

March's eyes suddenly hardened. 'So you knew Charles Peel, the driver?'

Jo nodded miserably. 'Oh, yes, I knew Charlie. He was my boyfriend at the time. I was supposed to be in the car that night, too, but I wouldn't set foot in it because Charlie was well over the limit. As usual. I did everything I could to make him see sense, even fought him physically for the keys, but we had such a blazing row he pushed me away and roared off in a rage to pick up a friend. I knew his friend as Red...' Jo halted, biting her lip.

CHAPTER FOUR

'THAT was the name my brother went by at Oxford.' March shook his head as though to clear it. 'You, of all people, are Jo Logan? My God! It never occurred to me that the missing link was a girl.' He took in a deep breath, his eyes suddenly arctic. 'After the accident I went to see the driver. But Charles Peel categorically denied knowing any man called Joe Logan—which was true, of course. You are not a man.'

'I don't blame you for feeling angry,' she said unhappily.

'I'm not angry, exactly. I just wish it hadn't been you,' he said harshly. 'In the end the police decided not to press charges, and young Peel was utterly frantic with anxiety about my brother, and so desperately guilt-ridden and penitent we felt he'd been punished enough.'

Jo smiled cynically. 'Charlie always did really great penitence.'

March frowned as he resumed his place on the sofa. 'That's very cold.'

'I speak from experience.' She gave a mirthless little laugh. 'If you'd tracked me down I would have given you a rather different take on the accident. I wondered why Charlie asked if anyone had been in touch with me. He tried to convince me that he'd turned over a new leaf. He even cried and swore he was on the wagon for keeps. But he'd done the dramatic penitent act before, so I didn't believe him.' Jo took in a deep breath. 'I haunted the hospital for a while, for information on how Red—your brother—was doing. I knew I couldn't get in to see him, but one of the girls on my staircase in college had a relation in Admissions there, who made enquiries for me and reported back. I was desperate to go home, but there was no way I could leave Oxford until I knew Red had been discharged.' She paused to look at March. 'Though I have no idea why he was muttering my name. I didn't know him very well. We weren't even in the same college.'

He shrugged. 'He seemed convinced you'd been in the car and injured, even killed. I suppose I should have asked later, but I was so damned relieved when he started getting better I couldn't risk prodding his memory into life in case it put him back to square one. And of course *I* knew there'd been no one else in the car.'

She shivered. 'I suffered agonies of guilt afterwards because I'd failed to get Charlie's keys away from him,'

'Were you in love with him?' asked March, surprising her.

Jo thought it over. 'It's hard to believe now,' she said wearily, 'but I thought I was at the time.' Her mouth turned down. 'I was straight out of a girls' school. Charlie was quite a bit older. If you met him you know he was rather good-looking. My head was turned when he singled me out. At first I thought his drinking was the usual student stuff, but it soon became obvious that Charlie was well on the way to becoming an alcoholic.'

'Were you lovers?'

Jo flushed. 'Not a word I would use. We did sleep together once or twice, but it was the first time for me and not—not very successful. All my fault, according to Charlie.'

March mouth tightened. 'The idiot's drink problem was to blame, not you. What happened to him afterwards?'

'I refused to return his calls after the accident, so he wrote to me eventually, saying he'd dried out in some clinic. He was starting work at Peel Plastics, a small company owned by his father. Charlie loathed the idea, but knew he had no hope of graduating after what had happened.' Jo's eyes dulled. 'Neither had I. He'd put an end to all possibility of that for me as well as himself.'

'And you wanted to graduate?'

'Of course I did! It was what I'd worked so hard for at school, and Jack and Kate were so proud when I got to Oxford.' Her mouth twisted in disgust. 'But I blew the whole thing. Someone made of sterner stuff than me would have stopped blaming Charlie, I suppose, and knuckled down to get a degree. But the whole Oxford experience was ruined for me—academically and every other way.'

March nodded slowly. 'It's dawned on me at last why you looked familiar the first time I spotted you. I must have seen you outside the hospital.'

'Very probably. I was there often enough.'

He frowned. 'When I referred to you as Miss Sutton, why the hell didn't you put me right there and then?'

Jo's colour rose. 'I had my reasons.'

He was silent for a while, eyeing her closely. 'Your name is Logan and your father is Jack. Would he, by any chance, be the moving force behind Logan Development?'

Her chin lifted. 'Yes.'

'Ah. Not just a builder, but a well-known developer and conservationist.'

'Yes.'

His eyes speared hers. 'You obviously didn't want me to know that your father is a wealthy man.'

Jo flushed guiltily. 'Do you blame me? It was my main attraction for Charlie. And for some of the male students on my business course.'

March eyed her in a silence that grew so prolonged and unbearable Jo was ready to scream by the time he broke it. 'So you were afraid a mere jobbing gardener like myself might also get ideas about the little rich girl?' he drawled, the words like shards of ice. He got to his feet, looking down his nose at her with such hostility she shrivelled inside. 'We haven't known each other long, but in my supreme vanity I thought you might have trusted me more than that. Have no fear. I'm not interested in your father's wealth—nor in you any more, if that's what you think of me,' he added bitterly. 'Goodbye.'

Goodbye? Jo listened in numb disbelief as March walked out of the room and out of the house. At the growl of his car engine, mortified colour rose in her face. So that was that, then. Finding out that she was Jo Logan had damped down March Aubrey's ardour pretty sharply. And, to top that, her reason for keeping her wealthy background secret had enraged him so much he had transformed into an implacable, arrogant stranger right before her eyes.

Jo got up early next morning, feeling like death warmed up. Her bathroom mirror confirmed that she looked like it. After a shower followed by hot coffee there was slight improvement, but Sunday lunch at Mill House was a prospect she just couldn't face for once.

'I've got the sniffles, Kate,' she fibbed. 'So I won't come round for lunch. A cold is the last thing you need right now.'

'Oh, darling, what bad luck. How did it go last night?'

'Very well,' lied Jo. 'My date was impressed. Molly was on top form.'

'Good. But I hate to think of you alone and sneezing today,' said Kate, sounding worried.

'I'm not that bad. In fact I might take my germs on a drive to Arnborough Hall again, and take in what I missed last time.'

'And catch up with your hot gardener while you're at it?'

When she reached the garden centre Jo wandered around the various displays of alpines and winter-flowering plants, had a look at the rose bushes and beautiful pot plants on sale, and wondered where the grafting house was. Not that she could imagine barging into it if she found out. If she met March by accident, fine. But even if she did he might look down his nose in that daunting way of his and tell her to get lost. The mere thought sent Jo hurrying from the garden centre to pay for another look round Arnborough Hall, where she found the same woman on duty in the Great Hall.

'Ah, hello again,' said the steward, smiling. 'You're back to see what you missed last time!'

Jo nodded. 'As you see, I came early today.'

'I'm afraid you've just missed a tour again, so you can either wait for the next in an hour, or go it alone.'

Jo had no interest in a tour. She went straight to the long gallery and the Victorian portraits, for a second look at the strangely familiar Baron. He'd been painted in formal evening dress, his red-gold hair and side whiskers luxuriant. The feeling of familiarity grew stronger as she went on to the teenage sons flanking him in smaller frames. Her eyes narrowed ominously as the penny finally dropped. She hadn't known Red very well, because Charlie had kept them apart from each other as much as possible. But she remembered him well enough to see that he was a dead ringer for the younger of the two haughty young men in the portraits.

Jo's heart sank as she faced the truth. If Red—Rufus—was in some way connected with the family, then obviously so was March. Though he looked nothing like these fair Anglo-Saxons. Maybe he was a half-brother, or illegitimate or something. Which would explain his job. Then her heart literally stopped for a moment in front a modern portrait of a beautiful young woman in formal evening dress, with a diamond tiara in her black hair and a smile in her very familiar eyes.

Jo turned as a voice spoke behind her.

'Lady Arnborough was the mother of the present Baron,' a steward told her.

'Really?' She cleared her throat. 'How interesting. Is there a portrait of her son anywhere?'

'Not as such. There are only photographic studies of the present generation.' The man ushered her towards an alcove, then left her to study the display at her leisure.

A formal posed wedding photograph of Lord and Lady Arnborough took pride of place above a trio of camera portraits taken when each of the subjects was eighteen, according to the captions. First the Honourable March Aubrey Clement, the heir, image of his mother. Then came the Honourable Henrietta Frances Clement, to the left below him, her features cast in the same mould, and alongside her the Honourable Rufus Randall Clement, with the fair colouring and features of his father, though with more sensitivity in his face than his handsome, forceful sire. Below the formal portraits a series of informal snapshots showed the Clement youngsters playing tennis, cricket, riding, picnicking, painting—and, in the heir's case, gardening.

Jo stood rooted to the spot as angry humiliation was swamped by a wave of bitter disappointment. She could have fallen in love with her hot gardener, but no chance of that with the high and mighty Lord Arnborough. She managed to thank the steward, then hurried downstairs and out through the vestibule, thankful that the friendly woman at the door to the Great Hall was too busy to notice as she escaped. Jo stormed along the paths between the lawns, and once through the gatehouse took to her heels. She sprinted down the winding road and on past the Arnborough Arms as though the devil were after her. But her long, headlong flight failed to shake off the resentment and embarrassment boiling away inside her. To think that March had actually had the gall to be annoyed because she'd kept her real name from him. What a laugh! Lord Arnborough, it appeared, had fancied a spot of incognito dalliance with one of the lower classes.

Jo forced herself to wait long enough to calm down before

beginning the drive home. No point in following Charlie Peel's example. But unlike him she was cold sober. Well, not cold, more like red hot. But sober. After an interval of deep breathing exercises she was about to get in the car when her phone rang. And she did go cold when she saw the caller.

'Grandpa?'

'Jack's taken Kate to the hospital, darling. I'm taking care of Kitty. Are you at home?'

'No. I'm at Arnborough Hall, but I'm starting back right now. I'll be with you as soon as I can.'

'Good, but don't rush. Drive carefully. Kitty's fine.'

'I'm on my way.'

It was a nightmare drive. Heavy rain added to Jo's stress factor after a mile or two, forcing her to drive carefully instead of rushing back to Mill House at top speed. The baby was three weeks early. Oh, God, she prayed, please take care of Kate. And the baby.

The rain had stopped by the time she turned down the long drive to Mill House. Kitty shot out to meet her, with Grandpa in pursuit.

'Jo—Jo,' cried the child as Jo leapt from the car. 'Mummy's gone to buy the baby.'

Jo's angst towards March was suddenly irrelevant. 'How very exciting,' she said, and picked the little girl up to hug her. 'And how are you, Grandpa?'

Tom smiled manfully. 'Fine, but since Jack went in the ambulance with Kate—'

'Ambulance?' Jo followed him into the hall and set Kitty down.

'Jack rang for one, afraid Kate might need attention on the journey. But now you're here can you cope if I go to the hospital and give Jack a lift home?' he asked anxiously.

'Yes, of course.' Jo's empty stomach tightened. 'What shall we do, Kitty-cat?'

'Draw pictures.'

'Right. Off you go then, Grandpa.' Jo smiled at him lovingly. 'Keep me posted.'

'I'll report as soon as I get there,' he promised.

The afternoon was the longest of Jo's life. Her grandfather rang as promised, to say that things were proceeding normally and he was staying on at the hospital as moral support for Jack.

'How is he?'

'In a bit of a state! By the way, Kate asked me to ring Anna. Can you do that?'

'Yes, of course. But ring me again soon.'

Kitty eventually got bored with drawing, and asked to see one of her cartoon films. Anything but *Bambi,* thought Jo with a shudder. Once the child was settled, she went to Jack's study to ring Kate's closest friend, Anna Maitland. She promised to ring again the moment there was any news, then went back to the kitchen and took Kitty on her lap to snuggle down together in the big armchair kept there for the purpose. When the film ended Kitty's lip trembled as she turned tearful eyes on her sister.

'I wish Mummy was here.'

So did Jo. 'I know, pet. But you'll have to make do with me instead tonight.'

Tom rang soon afterwards, to say things were proceeding as before, and that Jack had left the labour ward long enough to swallow some coffee before rushing back to Kate. 'I'll ring you again soon,' Tom promised.

Jo enlisted Kitty's help to make supper, then sat with the child as she ate, trying to console herself with the reminder that Kate had done this twice before. But the thought of her mother in agonising labour was unbearable. If this is the end result, thought Jo in anguish, no consuming passion for me.

Afterwards, it took a lot of cajoling from Jo to get Kitty into a bath and put her to bed.

'Want Mummy,' wailed the child piteously as Jo sat on the bed with her.

'I know, darling, so do I,' said Jo, surprising her little sister.

'But you're a big girl!'

'Even big girls need their Mummies sometimes,' Jo assured her.

Amazed by such weakness from a girl as big as her sister, Kitty agreed to listen to one of her longer stories, and to Jo's infinite relief fell asleep before the end of it.

Jo was on her way downstairs to make herself some much needed tea when her phone rang again. 'Grandpa?' she said eagerly.

'Afraid not, Joanna. It's March. Dan told me he'd seen you running past the pub earlier, on your way to the car park. Did you come to see me?'

In his dreams! 'Absolutely not. I can't talk now. My mother's in hospital and I'm waiting for news.'

'The baby?'

'Yes.'

'In that case I'll get off the line at once and call you tomorrow.'

'Please don't put yourself to the trouble—Lord Arnborough.' Jo snapped her phone shut and hurried back to Kitty, who'd begun to wail.

Tom rang twice during the endless evening, but only to report that Kate was still in labour. It was midnight when the phone rang again, and at last it was Jack—hoarse and triumphant.

'Darling, you've got a little brother, all seven pounds of him, and your wonderful, marvellous mother is exhausted, but she's come through it safely. Thank God—'

His voice cracked on the last, and Jo heaved in a shaky breath, wanting to cry her eyes out with relief. 'Oh Jack, I'm so *relieved*. Are you coming home now?'

'As soon as Kate is settled for the night. Have you had a rough time with Kitty?'

'She's been wanting her mummy.' Jo's voice thickened. 'So have I.'

'For God's sake don't cry, or I will, too. And Dad's had enough on his plate tonight without that!'

Jo managed a chuckle. 'Poor Grandpa.'

When the men got home there was much kissing and hugging and reports on Kate's well-being. Jo rang Anna Maitland very briefly, while Jack went up to check on his sleeping daughter, then whipped up a midnight feast of soup and toast and mugs of tea.

'It should be champagne,' said Jack, yawning, 'but if I even sniff the cork I'll keel over.'

'So what's he like, this new brother of mine?' demanded Jo. 'Does he have any hair? Is he like Kitty?'

'At the moment he's bald, with a chubby red face, and he looks like himself!'

Tom laughed. 'Has he got a name yet?'

'Oh, yes,' said Jack casually. 'We've had names ready for months. Margaret Joanna for a girl, and Thomas John for a boy.'

Jo's throat thickened at the look on her grandfather's face. 'Perfect,' she said huskily.

She was settling down in her old room before she allowed herself to think of the phone call from March. Or Lord Arnborough, she reminded herself acidly. A good thing she'd found out now, before things went any further. March was a man she could have grown to care for in an adult way very different from the fleeting teenage infatuation she'd felt for Charlie. But he'd walked out on her anyway, so there was no possibility of that—whatever his name was…

Jo woke with a start as Kitty burst in the room next morning with big news. Her excitement about the new baby was intense. She was going to see him later, with Daddy, and did Jo know that you didn't buy babies? God sent them to you in the hospital. But she wished the baby was a girl.

'God had already sent Mummy two girls, darling,' she pointed out. 'He wanted her to have a boy this time.'

'I told Daddy to ask for a girl next time.' Kitty sighed. 'But he said there wasn't going to *be* a next time.'

Amen to that, thought Jo with feeling, and jumped out of bed. 'Come on, Kitty-cat—time to get dressed. Hazel will be here soon—you can tell *her* all about the baby.'

Hazel Carter, mother of Molly and a great favourite of Kitty's, had worked for the Logans for years, and still preferred to help Kate with the running of Mill House rather than wait on tables in her daughter's restaurant.

'Thank God for Hazel,' said a very haggard Jack at the breakfast table. 'If she just sees to Kitty for a day or two—that's all I ask. To hell with the house.'

'When she gets here, go back to bed for a bit,' advised Jo. 'I'll go home to change, then drive into the office to spread the news and keep things ticking over. But I'm taking a long lunch hour, boss—to visit Kate.'

Jack got up to hug her. 'Thank you, Jo. Though you must be tired too. Knock off early today.'

'I'll see how I get on.' She kissed Kitty's butter-smeared cheek. 'See you later, poppet.'

Jo's morning passed with constant interruption. Once she'd announced the arrival of Thomas John Logan, she had visits from staff eager to pass on their congratulations. By the time Jo was ready to leave for the hospital she was in possession of a huge bouquet of flowers, several cuddly toys and, from her female colleagues, a pile of magazines and a basket of French toiletries.

'Goodness,' said Kate, once Jo had left off hugging her to look in the crib beside the bed. 'What a haul!'

'And none of it from me.' Jo smiled down at the pink sleeping face. 'Gosh, he's chunky.' She looked up at Kate, who looked tired and pale, but otherwise better than Jo had expected. 'Was it a battle to produce him, Kate?'

'It wasn't a walk in the park, certainly, but he's worth it.'
Kate smiled indulgently. 'Wild horses wouldn't make Jack
admit it, but I think he's secretly delighted to have a son.'

Jo shook her head vehemently. 'He's just delighted that
you're both safe, believe me. Kitty, however, would have preferred a sister.'

Kate laughed. 'She'll be fine once she actually sees the
baby. Jack's bringing her in with Grandpa this afternoon. How
is Tom, by the way?'

'He was very tired last night—but, Kate, you should have
seen his face when Jack told him the baby's name!'

'But his grandson's not to be Tommy. He must be Tom, too.
By the way,' added Kate, 'Hazel's happy to move in with us for
as long as I want, which is good.'

'What can *I* do to help?'

'Just see that things run smoothly at the firm, darling, so Jack
can spend more time at home for a bit.'

'I'll be only too glad to,' Jo assured her, then bent to kiss her
mother. 'You'd better take a nap before your next visitors arrive.
How long will you be here?'

'I might be home tomorrow.'

When Jo had finished for the night she drove straight to Mill
House, to find Jack and Tom enjoying a drink in the kitchen
while Hazel prepared dinner. Kitty ran to her sister joyfully, full
of her visit to Mummy and little Tom.

'He's so little, Jo!'

'He'll soon grow.' Jo smiled warmly at Hazel. 'Thank you
for moving in.'

'I'm only too glad to. It's a change from living on my own.'
She eyed Jo closely. 'You look as if a good rest wouldn't do
you any harm, dear. Are you staying for dinner?'

'Actually, if you've got everything in hand, Hazel, I'd rather
go back to Park Crescent. Is that all right, Jack?'

He nodded. 'Of course. Do you want to come in with me tonight, to see Kate?'

She shook her head. 'Tell her I'll pop in tomorrow lunch-time again.'

'Make sure you eat something,' said her father severely. 'Have you got any food at your place?'

'How about some of this chicken casserole?' said Hazel. 'I made loads.'

'Hazel, you are a godsend,' said Jo thankfully.

'Want you to stay here,' said Kitty, scowling.

'Jo needs to go home to her house and rest tonight,' said Jack firmly.

'But I want her to read a story!'

'I can do that,' said Tom promptly, and Kitty stared at him in astonishment.

'Can you *read*, Grandpa?'

'Oh, yes. Even the big words,' he assured her, ignoring the smothered mirth from the others.

'In that case,' said Jo, grinning, 'I'll take off and get some ironing done before supper.'

When she got home a message was waiting on her answer-machine.

'Joanna, it's March. I haven't rung today in case you needed your line free for emergencies, but I'm anxious for news of your mother. I doubt that you'll ring me back, so I'll try again later.'

Jo eyed the machine coldly and got on with the ironing. She was putting the iron away when March rang again. She clenched her teeth as his deep, drawling tones left more or less the same message as before, then turned her back on the telephone and went up to have a bath. She was in her dressing gown, wet hair swathed in a towel, when the doorbell rang. Her heart leapt, then righted itself again as she ran downstairs to the hall. March— or Lord Arnborough, to give him his proper title, she thought viciously—was tall enough to be seen through the fanlight. It wasn't him. And it wasn't Jack, either, for the same reason.

Jo opened the door very cautiously, then grinned as she saw familiar sandy curls and hefty shoulders. 'Hi, Leo. Long time no see.'

'No have time off,' he groaned. 'Are you going to let me in?'

Jo opened the door wide. 'Are you hungry?'

Leo's open, friendly face looked hurt. 'I come here for reasons other than mere food, Jo Logan.'

She made a mental note to ask people to call her Joanna from now on. 'My apologies, Doctor.'

'Actually, I'm on my way out to dine with the parents before I fall into bed for a day or three.' He grinned. 'I called in to congratulate you. Josh's squeeze in Maternity told him your mother delivered a baby boy yesterday. How about coffee to celebrate, so I keep awake at the wheel on my way to Chez Carey?'

'Come with me to the kitchen, my friend. Coffee you shall have.'

'So your father has a son at last,' said Leo, as they sat down at the kitchen table.

'All he wanted in life was Kate safe through the birth and a healthy baby,' said Jo severely. 'The sex didn't matter to him.'

'Sex doesn't matter to me any more, either,' said Leo morosely, and yawned. 'If I ever get a girl into bed again I'll have forgotten what to do.'

Jo gave a snort of laughter. 'Don't worry. It's supposed to be like riding a bike—you never forget.'

'Glad to hear it.' He eyed her in a professional manner. 'You look a bit frazzled. Too much socializing, or just not sleeping well?'

'Sunday left its mark on me. On top of worrying about Kate I had the job of keeping Miss Katherine Logan entertained!' Jo got rid of the towel and ran her fingers through her hair.

Leo whistled in sympathy. 'No wonder you look fragile. What does our Kitty-cat think of her baby brother?'

'Wrong sex, but cute. Are you sure you won't have a sandwich or something?'

'Better not. Mother's roasting the fatted calf as we speak, so the prodigal had better be on his way to eat it.' Leo drained his mug and got to his feet, rubbing a hand over his tired young face. On the way to the door he gave her a hug. 'Great to see you, Jo. As soon as I can I'll take you out to supper for a change.'

'I'll hold you to that.' Jo looked up as the doorbell rang, and saw the top of a dark head through the fanlight. 'That'll be Jack on his way home.' She opened the door, then wished she hadn't. Her second visitor of the night was Lord Arnborough.

CHAPTER FIVE

MARCH looked at her in silence for a moment, then said, 'Good evening, Joanna,' in a tone so forbidding it raised her hackles. What right had *he* to be angry? 'I left two messages on your machine without success, so I took a chance on finding you in.' Cold gold eyes took in Jo's dressing gown and bare feet, then lingered on Leo's arm, which was still firmly round her waist. He held out a hand. 'March Clement.'

Leo dropped his arm to shake hands, smiling cheerfully. 'Hi—Leo Carey.' He kissed Jo's cheek. 'Must dash, love. By the way, birth weight and name, please. Mother's hot on that kind of thing.'

'Seven pounds,' said Jo. 'And he's Thomas John. Enjoy the fatted calf, then, and come again soon.'

'Will do.' He nodded to March, who stood aside to hold the door for him. 'Goodnight all.'

March closed the door and stood with his back to it. He wore a leather jacket and jeans as well worn as young Dr Carey's, and a look on his face she objected to. 'I apologise for intruding,' he said at last, breaking the hostile silence.

'Why did you?' she said stonily.

'After my lack of success with the telephone it seemed the only option.' His eyes held hers. 'Did you get my messages?'

'Yes.'

'But you didn't pick up. Why?'

'Isn't that obvious?'

'Tell me anyway.'

'I didn't want to speak to you.' She shrugged. 'I still don't, Lord Arnborough.'

His mouth twisted. 'It's just a title, Joanna. I'm still the same man.'

'Rubbish,' she spat at him with sudden heat. 'You're the umpteenth Baron Arnborough. And I assume the "sort of flat" you live in is a suite of apartments roped off from the public at the Hall. No wonder you laughed when I said I'd like to marry the heir! But now you *are* here, put me straight.'

He moved closer. 'About what?'

'Why did you lie?'

'The same reason you did, Joanna. I wanted someone to like me for myself, not for my blasted title and my stately home.' His eyes hardened. 'Just as you kept *your* name secret in case I fancied your father's money more than you.'

Jo shivered, suddenly aware of bare feet and cold tiled floor.

March startled her by picking her up. She stiffened like a board as he carried her into the parlour and put her down on the sofa. 'Your feet must be freezing.' He would have chafed them, but Jo had curled them up under the robe in knee-jerk rejection. 'So how did you find out?' he demanded, standing back.

'On my first visit to—to your home,' she began, 'your Victorian forebears looked familiar. They reminded me of someone. So on Sunday I drove back to the Hall and went straight to the portrait gallery. I realised that the someone was your brother. Further on I saw the portrait of your mother, and then a photograph of the heir at eighteen—the Honourable March Aubrey Clement himself. You were a handsome lad,' she added.

He shrugged. 'Hetty and I take after our mother, Rufus after the male line—though he's the first to have artistic leanings, and he was delicate as a child. Father wanted Rufus to study

Land Management like me, so he could pitch in and do his share one day. But in the end Rufus had his own way and did his Fine Art course. By that time I was working for a Home Counties firm, looking after other people's venerable buildings. But when my father died I returned home and buckled down to the full-time job of looking after my own.'

'That must take some doing,' she said stiffly.

'It's a full-time occupation,' he agreed. 'Like so many of my breed, my assets far exceed my cash flow. By the time my father inherited, the Hall was in a pretty bad way. But with various grants and the agricultural returns from the family acres he started up a restoration programme that's still going on to some extent.' He smiled wryly. 'Father also had the great good fortune to marry a lady who not only possessed intelligence and beauty, but a wealthy father. So at times of crisis through the years my grandfather gave a helping hand.' He raised an eyebrow as the doorbell rang. 'Are you expecting more visitors?'

'No,' said Jo, jumping up. 'I'm not.' She hurried into the hall and groaned as she saw the familiar outline through the fanlight. 'It's my father.' Heart sinking, she opened the door to Jack, who looked at her bare feet in disapproval which changed to outright hostility when he saw the man behind her.

'Am I interrupting something?' he demanded.

Jo shook her head. 'What's the matter? You look terrible.' She seized his arm. 'Is something wrong with Kate?'

'Look, I'll go,' said March.

'You're the gardener,' said Jack suddenly.

March nodded. 'My name's Clement. How do you do?'

'Never mind all that,' said Jo impatiently. 'What's wrong, Jack?'

'Could we sit down somewhere?' he said wearily. 'And some coffee before I drive home would be good. Only put something on your feet, please, Jo. And don't worry, there's nothing wrong exactly. Kate needs a blood transfusion before she can come home. They'd started it before I got there tonight. It gave me a hell of a shock. And the baby was missing. He'd been taken off to the nursery.'

'If you two will go into the parlour I'll put some coffee on,' said Jo, willing March to refuse and just leave. Instead he held the door open for Jack and followed him into the parlour.

Jo flew into the kitchen to deal with the coffee-maker, then ran upstairs to pull on jeans and a sweater and thrust her feet into shoes. She ran a comb through her hair and tore back downstairs to set a tray, then took it into the parlour.

'Can I get you something to eat, Jack?' Jo asked as she filled cups.

'No, thanks, darling. I just called in to warn you in case Kate is still hooked up to the transfusion gear when you see her tomorrow.' He drank some coffee and took a look at March. 'So you work at Arnborough?'

'Actually, Jack,' said Jo acidly, 'he owns the place. He's *Lord* Arnborough.'

'Something, as you can tell, that your daughter takes objection to,' said March, and drank the coffee she'd given him so grudgingly.

Jack eyed first March, then Jo, looking as though he was too tired to take it in. 'Why do you object, Jo?'

'Because I didn't tell her that from the first,' March informed him. 'Just as Joanna forgot to tell *me* her name was Logan.'

Jack nodded sagely. 'She didn't want you to know I'm her father.'

'You look hardly old enough, sir,' said March politely.

'I'm more than old enough to be Joanna's father, but nothing like old enough to be called sir by someone your age!' said Jack dryly, and gave Jo his cup. 'That was a lifesaver, but now I'd better be on my way.' He got up, looking at March steadily. 'I'm not sure we'll meet again, but it was interesting to make your acquaintance.'

'I hope to further it,' said March, returning the look in kind.

'From the expression on my daughter's face, you'll need to work on that,' said Jack, and yawned. 'Sorry. I need my bed.' He put his arms round Jo. 'Don't overdo things tomorrow.'

'All right, Dad. Go home and get some sleep.' Jo coloured at the arrested look in her father's eyes, but he merely nodded coolly to March as he went out.

Jo shut the parlour door very deliberately as she followed her father into the hall.

'Dad?' said Jack, smoothing her hair.

'Does that make you feel too old?'

'It makes me feel quite wonderful,' he assured her, and kissed her nose.

'Good. Now, get some sleep. And don't worry. I'll keep things ticking over at the office tomorrow before I take off to see Kate.'

'Don't you mean Mum?' he said slyly.

Jo shook her head. 'She's still my lovely Kate—as she always has been.'

'Mine, too.' He kissed her cheek and opened the door. 'Should I stay to see His Lordship off the premises?'

Her eyes glittered. 'No, thanks. I reserve that pleasure for myself.'

March was standing where she'd left him. 'Before I leave,' he began, forestalling her, 'I insist on giving you some idea of what my life entails.'

'Since we're unlikely to meet again, it's of no interest to me,' lied Jo.

His jaw clenched. 'For God's sake, Joanna, you'd think I'd committed murder. Put your knife away and listen. I just wanted to be plain old March, enjoying time with a beautiful girl who seemed to like me for myself.'

'It's amazing your cover wasn't blown that first night in

the pub,' she pointed out, ignoring a slight lift at the 'beautiful girl' bit.

'I asked Dan not to let the cat out of the bag. The locals know me, of course, but I pass unnoticed among the customers at the garden centre. And that's the way I like it.' He smiled. 'Normally I rush through at the place as quickly as possible, but then that day I saw you—a life-changing moment.'

Jo steeled herself against the smile. 'If you must put me in the picture, stick to the facts, please.'

'Certainly.' His eyes hardened. 'I run the Hall with a bare minimum of staff. One part-time administrator deals with bookings and publicity, a rota of twenty-five stewards and guides deal with visitors, and a small team of locals work part-time to do the actual cleaning. The only full-time workers are my housekeeper, Mrs Dean, and the gardener, Ed Pargeter, of whom you have heard much already. And there's myself, of course. My father had my mother to help him, but I don't possess such an advantage. So as you see,' he added, 'Lord Arnborough's life is not all fun and games. Can you blame him for wanting time off now and again?'

'Not in the least.' Her eyes flashed. 'But I felt such a fool for worrying that you couldn't afford a meal at Molly's. I even made dinner for you at home so you wouldn't be embarrassed if I paid when we went out.'

His eyes softened. 'It was a wonderful dinner. And such a pleasure to eat it with you, in this little gem of a house, without a suit of armour or an ancestral portrait in sight.'

'If you feel like that why don't you make Arnborough over to the National Trust?' she asked, then quailed at the sudden blaze in his eyes.

'It's my *home*, Joanna. The National Trust was never an option. And even if it were,' he added, 'they can't act without an endowment.'

'So how do you manage to carry on?'

'By finding ways of bringing in income. The garden centre is a big success, thank God—and Ed. It also provides employment locally. But a film producer for a brother-in-law is a plus. Due to him Arnborough is listed on appropriate websites and registers as available for use as a location, both indoors and out. It's an excellent source of income. Fashion magazines and companies who make films or television series about the Tudors or the Stuarts, or dramatise yet another Jane Austen or Brontë story, regularly pay good money to use Arnborough.'

'So that explains the feeling I had there,' said Jo, deeply disappointed. 'Every room looked so familiar, as though I'd been there before in another life. But I'd merely seen it on film.'

March nodded. 'I was sure you'd found me out that first night, when you said you'd looked at the portraits in the gallery. But luck was with me.'

'Because I left after the Victorian section. If I hadn't we wouldn't have seen each other again,' she added, and felt a thump under her ribs as their eyes met.

'That,' he said very deliberately, 'would have been a tragedy.' He took her hands. 'So, Joanna, are we friends again?' He smiled with his usual gleaming confidence, so obviously sure of her answer Jo's inner rebel rose up in arms.

'Now I know who you are that's just not possible between us. We have nothing in common,' she said tartly, and pulled her hands away. 'You and I inhabit two totally different worlds, Lord Arnborough.'

'And never the twain shall meet?' His eyes blazed with such anger she backed away involuntarily.

'Yes.'

March straightened, suddenly so physically formidable it was hard for Jo to stand her ground. 'I see,' he said curtly. 'In that case I'll stop wasting my time—and yours.'

And without another word he strode from the room and out

of the house for the second time, leaving her incandescent with fury because he'd made no attempt to change her mind.

Jo stood where he'd left her, in the middle of the room, waiting to hear the growl of his car engine. But in the end she gave up and made for the kitchen. The doorbell rang before she got there, and she ran along the hall, her heart leaping about like a mad thing when she saw who it was.

'Forgotten something?' she demanded, as she opened the door to March.

'Yes,' he said, and picked her up, kicking the door shut behind him. 'This.' He smothered her furious protests with his mouth as he carried her into the parlour and sat on the sofa, holding her fast on his lap.

Hissing like an angry cat, Jo tried to get free, but March caught her flailing hands and closed his arms round her like iron bands as he kissed her until they were both panting like long-distance runners.

'To hell with friendship. I'm going to be your lover. And the only thing we need in common for that is *this*.' To remove all possible doubt he began kissing her again, but this time he caressed her with clever, fire-raising hands while his lips and tongue worked magic. But at the very moment when Jo was melting into hot, boneless response, ready to do anything he wanted, March raised his head to look down into her eyes.

'You drove me to that,' he said through his teeth. 'I've never used force on a woman in my life before.'

Because women normally dropped into his waiting hands like ripe plums, thought Jo, utterly disgusted with herself because she'd almost done the same. Even more mortifying, there was a strong possibility she still might if he tried the same tactics again.

'Let me up now, please,' she said, proud of herself because her voice was steady.

March slackened his hold and helped her to her feet. 'If I

hurt you, I apologise,' he said shortly, and looked her in the eye. 'But I won't lie and say I'm sorry for the rest.'

'You're honest,' she conceded.

'We aristocrats try our best,' he said with biting sarcasm, and made for the door. He turned to look at her. 'Having received what I came for, Miss Logan, I'll bid you goodnight and never darken your door again.' His eyes stabbed hers. 'And this time I mean it.'

This was the last thing Jo wanted. She tried to find some way to tell him that without losing face, and in the end—to her own surprise as much as his—asked him if he'd eaten.

'No,' March said blankly. 'Are you by any chance offering to feed me?'

'Fool that I am, yes,' she said irritably. 'But it's just a kitchen supper,' she warned.

March drew himself up to his full height, looking down his nose at her with all the hauteur of the portraits in his long gallery. 'You're asking me to sit at your kitchen table?' he drawled with disdain, then dropped the pose and gave her the smile that turned her knees to jelly. 'I'd like nothing better.'

'In that case,' she said, as they went into the kitchen, 'sit there, so you don't get in my way, and I'll give you things to do.'

'Yes, ma'am!' March slung his jacket over the back of one of her chairs and sat down, his pleasure so obvious at the unexpected turn of events she thawed completely.

Jo passed him silverware and mats and told him to lay the table. 'If you know how,' she added.

'Of course I know how! I live alone, remember.'

'In a "sort of flat",' she agreed wryly, filling a kettle. 'How big is it?'

'Big enough. Some of it,' he went on, 'was the domain of the servants at one time. My mother had a good eye, and with the help of an architect friend of my father managed to achieve comfortable living quarters for us without losing the character of the old rooms. What else can I do?' he added.

Jo put the casserole to heat in the microwave, and then handed March a board, a loaf and a bread knife. 'You can cut some of that.' In record time she set two steaming plates on the table and sat down. 'There. No serving dishes tonight,' she informed him pointedly.

March ate in silence for a moment, looking across at her. 'I can't help who I am, Joanna.'

'No.' She sighed. 'It's just that I felt like such a fool when I found out.'

'You weren't straight with me either,' he pointed out. 'It got me on the raw that you thought I'd be some kind of sponging hanger-on if I heard about your background.'

She coloured slightly. 'It's happened before, so you can understand why.'

'I do. The same goes for my little deception,' he countered.

'It's a whole lot bigger than mine,' said Jo, taking a slice of bread. 'I don't have a title, or ancestors who fought in the Civil War.'

His eyes narrowed. 'But there's something mysterious about you, just the same. If you were adopted, do you know who your real parents were?'

'Oh, yes. One day, when—if—I get to know you better, I'll tell you about them.'

'*When*, not if,' said March flatly. 'I'm damned if I'll let an accident of birth prevent a relationship between us, Joanna.'

'Accident?'

'I just happened to be born to a father with a title.'

'Was his name March, too?'

He shook his head. 'My grandfather's. Mother was the only child of Randall Lewis March, an old rogue of an entrepreneur with a finger in every profitable pie going.'

Jo eyed him questioningly. 'She must have died young.'

'Just after my finals.' His eyes shadowed. 'My father was never the same afterwards.'

'Poor man.' Impulsively Jo reached out a hand to touch his. 'You must have suffered, too, March.'

'All three of us did. But Rufus most of all because he was the youngest—her baby boy, as Mother used to tease him.' March shivered slightly. 'She had an emergency appendix operation that went wrong. It happened so suddenly we were all in shock afterwards, including my grandfather. He died not long afterwards.' He released her hand. 'Sorry, Joanna. You don't need this right now, when you look so tired. Have you had a bad day?'

'Bad night.' She looked him in the eye. 'I was hurt when you stormed off on Saturday night.'

'So was I.'

'Were you?'

'Yes. That's why I lost it.' He smiled a little. 'So, did our fight make your day harder for you? There must be more for you to do while your father's away.'

'There are plenty of people to keep things moving until the boss gets back to work. Including me.' Jo smiled proudly. 'But Jack is the driving force. Even so, I hope he'll stay home as long as Kate needs him.'

'He looks very young to be your father.'

'Jack's not even fifty yet, and so far no grey hair. But if you think *he* looks young you should see Kate!'

'I'd like to very much,' he said promptly. 'Or does meeting your mother come under the same heading of "not until you know me better"?'

Jo looked at him in thoughtful silence. 'Look, March,' she said at last, 'now I know who you are it's just so hard for me to see that happening.'

'Because of the blasted title,' he snapped, and got up so suddenly the table rocked. 'I can't change it, Joanna. I am who I am.'

'I know that!' Jo leapt up in consternation. 'Please don't storm off again.'

'Why not?'

She glared at him resentfully. 'You could at least try a little more persuasion.'

Suddenly very still, March raised an unsettling eyebrow. 'If I do resort to persuasion, Miss Logan, it might not be to your taste.'

'Try me.'

He held out his hand, his eyes bright with something that set her heart thudding. Aware that she could hardly complain after throwing down the gauntlet, Jo took the hand cautiously, half expecting to be jerked into his arms again. But March merely led her to the parlour and drew her down on the sofa beside him. He looked down into her wary face for a long moment, then took her in his arms and kissed her very thoroughly. At the first touch of his lips all her anger and indignation vanished, and she leaned into him, returning the kiss with warmth he accepted like a gift, his arms tightening as the kiss rapidly grew more heated.

'Is this the kind of persuasion you meant?' he demanded against her mouth.

'Not exactly,' she whispered. 'But I like it.'

He gave a smothered laugh, then kissed her again, his exploring tongue caressing hers. She shivered as his hands slid beneath her shirt, fingers outspread on her ribs just short of her breasts. She tensed, waiting, but his hands stayed still, the mere touch of them on her skin sending fire down to the part of her in full contact with his arousal.

March raised his head, breathing hard as he looked down into her eyes. 'You are so lovely, Joanna Logan. I don't know what my friendly persuasion is doing for you, but it's playing hell with me.'

'Then that had better be enough for now,' she said, and forced herself to stand up.

March got up with her and caught her close. 'You do realise I've wanted to kiss you senseless since the first time I saw you?'

Jo's lips twitched. 'Still not beating about the bush.'

'I am. Because I want a hell of a lot more. As,' he added dryly, 'I'm sure you could tell.' He smoothed her hair back from her face. 'But pride—or pig-headedness, if you like—is part of the package with this famous pedigree of mine. Send me away this time, Joanna, and I won't come back.'

She bit her lip, knowing he meant every word. And suddenly the thought of never seeing him again was so intolerable it simplified everything. 'I'm not sending you away,' she said abruptly.

His eyes gleamed with triumph. 'You've changed your mind?'

'Yes.'

'Why?'

'Because I like you, Lord Arnborough, even if you were a touch economical with the truth.'

'So were you, Miss Logan,' he retorted. 'I like you too—so much that I don't want to go. But perhaps I should, while I'm winning.'

'And is winning very important to you?'

'Of course. It is to every man.' March tightened his arms round her. 'But I want a lot more than mere friendship—in time.'

So do I, thought Jo. A couple of brief sessions in his arms had shown her that all too clearly. 'I can live with that,' she said, and gasped as his arms tightened enough to threaten risk to her ribs. 'At least,' she added with difficulty, 'I might if you let me breathe.'

He chuckled, and released her slowly. 'Joanna, I know your life is hectic at the moment, but I want to spend more time with you. Soon.'

'At the weekend?'

'Will you drive to Arnborough?'

Jo raised an eyebrow. 'I thought you didn't want me there again.'

'Only while I was incognito.' March smoothed a hand down her cheek. 'Now the gloves are off, so to speak, I thought you might like to see over the house with me. If you come early on Saturday we can explore before the paying public arrives.'

Her eyes sparkled. 'Will you show me the bits roped off from the public? Including your "sort of flat"?'

'Everything,' he promised.

'Then I'll come. I've already paid the entrance fee twice, by the way, so do I get in free this time?'

He leered theatrically. 'There might possibly be a small charge—but it won't be money.'

'La, sir!' She fluttered her eyelashes. 'What can you mean?'

'Exactly what you think I mean,' he said, and kissed her.

Jo responded with fervour, leaning into him as he held her close. She was no stranger to being kissed, but this was different. When March raised his head at last she told him so.

'Why different?' he demanded, his eyes narrowed to gleaming slivers of amber.

'Maybe because I haven't been kissed by a lord before.'

'In that case,' he drawled, 'I'd better make sure it's a memorable experience.'

Jo found a pleasure in just kissing she had never experienced before. In the past it had always been a prelude, usually brief, to what the man in question hoped would happen next. But March took infinite pleasure in teaching her the joy to be found in only the play of lips and tongue, of kisses which roamed all over her face, and then homed in again on the mouth which responded to his with such all-out fervour March groaned at last and buried his face in her hair

'I should go,' he muttered. 'Before I lose the territory I regained.'

'Are we having a battle, then?' Jo demanded.

He raised his head to look down at her. 'If so, victory is mine.'

She smiled wryly. 'But it's a good thing you didn't run into me at the Hall on Sunday. Once I saw your photograph I was ready to do murder.'

'Which would be a pity,' he said lightly, shifting her more comfortably. 'Rufus has no intention of marrying, he tells me. So the only hope of succession lies with me.'

'Then why haven't you lined up some aristocratic fiancée, ready to carry on the family name for you?' Jo paused, eyeing him narrowly. 'Or maybe you have.'

'At present, Joanna Logan, I have not.' March's eyes held hers steadily. 'I did at one time. She was beautiful, came from the same background—everything I'd ever wanted in a wife. I was crazy about her at the time. Like a fool I believed that my sentiments were returned when she said yes to my proposal. But when the lady discovered just how little hard cash went with the rest, my ancestral home—and my person—suddenly lost their charm.'

'Were you hurt?'

'Of course I was—not least my pride. So I decided to avoid anything remotely like that kind of relationship in future.'

Jo eyed him curiously. 'But there must have been other women in your life since then?'

'Of course. I'm no monk. But light-hearted, no-strings en-counters have been the order of the day since Lavinia.' March eyed her curiously. 'How about you? Anyone since young Peel?'

'Of course. I was a student at college here as well as Oxford, remember? But I steered clear of anything heavy. Unlike you, I've never suffered from a consuming passion, and I hope to keep it that way. These days I feel happiest socialising with girl-friends, or with the Carey twins.'

March drew her nearer. 'You could be happy socialising with me, too, Joanna.'

She smiled. 'I know I could. So I'll drive over to look round your home with you at the weekend.'

'You said you liked the place,' he reminded her.

'I do.' She frowned as something occurred to her. 'But tell me something. If you're family's so old, how come you're still just a baron?'

March gave a shout of laughter. 'You were throwing my title at me like a dirty word earlier—now it's not good enough for you?'

Jo grinned. 'I meant, Lord Arnborough, that I thought a family as old as yours would have risen to a higher rank at some point.'

'Ah, but we batted for Parliament during the Civil War.'

'No!' She stared at him, fascinated. 'How extraordinary. I pictured you as a Cavalier.'

March shook his head. 'Josiah Clement, the Lord Arnborough of the time, was Puritan to the core, and a respected politician. He did his utmost to help settle the differences between the opposing sides. He was no fan of Charles the First, but disagreed vehemently with regicide. He refused to endorse the sovereign's execution, declined a seat in Cromwell's parliament later, and afterwards lived in seclusion until Charles the Second came to the throne. At which point Josiah was pardoned, given a seat in the new parliament, and allowed to retain his barony. And barons we've been ever since.'

'Do you ever feel weighed down by all that history?' asked Joanna.

'It's just part of who I am,' he said, shrugging, and got up. 'And now, Miss Logan, I'll take myself off and let you get to bed.'

'I'm glad you came back,' she confided, as she went with him to the door.

'So am I. I hope you find your mother well tomorrow.' March bent his head and kissed her. 'Come early on Saturday morning,' he ordered, and smiled.

CHAPTER SIX

NEXT day Jo found Kate sitting by her hospital bed, giving her son milk.

'You look so much better,' Jo said fervently, kissing her. 'Is your blood count right back to normal?'

'It certainly is. But not my milk supply—the same as with you and Kitty. So it's the bottle for young Tom here, too.' Kate smiled. 'Jack's coming in an hour to take us home. Poor darling—he got the shock of his life last night when he saw me hooked up to the blood transfusion.'

'I know. He called in at Park Crescent to warn me. And met my hot gardener, by the way.'

'Really?' Kate's eyes sparkled as she patted her son against her shoulder. 'Were you feeding him again?'

'I hadn't intended to, but in the end I did.' Jo took the chair on the other side of the bed. 'March arrived while Leo Carey was there, and was noticeably uptight about it. Not that he had any right to be. *He* was the transgressor.'

Kate's eyes widened. 'Really? What had he done? Or shouldn't I ask?'

'Jack knows already.' Jo gave a crow of delight as the baby gave a loud burp. 'Oh, well done—clever boy,' she said, stroking the downy little head. 'Plug him into his bottle again and I'll tell you what happened last Sunday.'

Kate listened, entranced, as Jo told her tale. 'How amazing! So why did Lord Arnborough come to see you last night?'

'Apparently the pub landlord saw me storming past the Arnborough Arms on Sunday and told March, who wanted to know why.' Jo pulled a face. 'I was furious because I felt like such a fool. I'd actually told him that first night in the pub that I liked the Hall so much I wanted to marry the heir.'

'No!' Kate shifted her son more comfortably and shot a sly look at her daughter. 'Would you still like to do that?'

'No way,' said Jo fiercely. 'Come on, Kate, discounting a dozen or so other reasons, can you see me as chatelaine of Arnborough Hall?'

'Even so, you like this man a lot?'

'Yes.'

'So are you going to see him again?'

'He's taking me round the Hall on Saturday, before the public pay to do the same. Only I get to see the places they don't.'

Kate frowned. 'So where are you going with this?'

Jo shrugged. 'I don't know. Last night he said he wants us to be friends *at least*. If not Lord Arnborough was leaving and wasn't coming back. And he meant it.'

'Did he mean friendship, or something more?'

Jo got up restlessly. 'He's a man, so I suppose he'll want something more. I quite like the idea too—and not because he has a title.'

'I know that! You were smitten when you thought he was just a hot gardener.'

'I wish he still was,' said Jo sadly. 'It would make life so much simpler.'

'He's still the same man.'

'That's what he said. But, Kate, the man has a pedigree a mile long, and a house he opens to the public!'

'Something tells me you're a little bit serious about him already.'

Jo sighed. 'Just a little bit.'

Kate got up and handed Jo her baby brother. 'Cuddle him for a minute while I get dressed. And don't you dare let Charlie Peel get in the way of this thing with March.'

'Well, since he almost killed March's brother he's very much in the way.' Jo walked up and down, her hand cupped around the tiny head against her breast. 'You know how I feel about the accident.'

Kate was silent for a moment as she packed the last of her belongings into a suitcase, then took her son from Jo. 'Listen to me, Joanna Logan. Charlie ruined life at Oxford for you. Don't let him ruin your relationship with March.'

'I'm not doing that,' said Jo, surprised. 'I was just cross with March because he didn't tell me who he was right at the beginning.'

'Neither did you.'

'It was hardly the same! My family tree is a mere sapling compared with his.'

'But it's good stock just the same, Joanna. You're capable, intelligent, a pleasure to look at, and you can even cook! Lord Arnborough would be jolly lucky to have you as his chatelaine.' Kate paused, smiling down as the baby began to object. 'Sorry, my lovely boy. Was Mummy shouting? I was just telling your sister she's good enough for any man.'

Jo rolled her eyes. 'Thank you, Mummy!'

Kate looked up at the sound of a familiar voice outside. She smiled radiantly as her husband came in. 'Are you ready to take us home?'

'You bet I am,' said Jack Logan, kissing her. 'You look so much better, darling—thank God. How do you feel?'

'Raring to go home.'

'Can't wait to take you there.' He touched a finger to his son's cheek, and turned to his daughter. 'And how are you today, Jo?'

'I'm fine.'

'What happened after I left last night?' He turned to his wife. 'You know Jo's been hobnobbing with the aristocracy?'

'Any reason why she shouldn't?' demanded Kate. 'Our daughter is good enough for anyone.'

Jack blinked in surprise. 'Of course she is, you tigress! I only asked because last night Jo was so hostile to the man.'

Jo shrugged. 'Only because he'd kept quiet about his title, Jack.'

Her father's eyes gleamed. 'I thought I was Dad now?'

'Only on special occasions.'

Kate looked up from arranging her son in his carry cot. 'What's this?'

'Our daughter actually called me Dad for the first time last night,' Jack told her. 'Though Jo's titled chum told me I don't look old enough to be her father.'

'Oho! Trying to get in your good books,' said Kate, laughing.

'So did you send him off with a flea in his ear, Jo?' demanded her father.

'No. I gave him some supper. After all,' she added defensively, 'he can't help having a title.'

'Ah! You like him.'

'Yes. Did you?'

Jack smiled. 'Actually, I did. But if you go on seeing him he'd better not have any *droit du seigneur* ideas in mind.'

'For heaven's sake! Besides,' she added, as an afterthought, 'it doesn't apply because I'm single. *Droit du seigneur* gave the lord first go in the sack with his vassal's bride.'

'Beautifully put,' said Kate, rolling her eyes. 'I'm so glad your education wasn't wasted. Right, then, Jack. Let's say our goodbyes to the staff and take our son home.'

'Before you take off, could I ask a favour?' asked Jo.

'Anything you want,' said Jack promptly. 'Does it involve money?'

'No, permission.' Jo hesitated, eyeing her parents in appeal. 'Would you mind if I told March my own story some time?'

Joanna had mixed feelings as she drove to Arnborough the following Saturday. She was going to look round his house, she told herself, not meet the family. But some of the part-time cleaners would be around, getting the place ready to open to the public later. They would naturally be curious about March's guest. And with that in mind she was wearing a black cashmere knit dress and suede boots—this year's birthday present—and last year's chestnut suede trench coat. Not that it mattered. March had seen her with damp hair, in a towelling dressing gown well past its sell-by date, so almost anything would be an improvement.

She scowled as she turned down the road to Arnborough. Did all this girly fussing mean she was falling for the man? If so, she could nip that in the bud right now. She was happy to be his friend, maybe even his lover, but only a fool would fall in love with a man who had no intention of doing the same.

This time Jo drove to the visitors' car park at the Hall. There was no one around when she walked through the gatehouse arch, hoisting her black suede tote. But as she crossed over the moat March, in heavy jersey and cords, came hurrying round the side of the building, looking so delighted to see her she smiled warmly.

'You came!' he said, and took her hands, kissing her on both cheeks.

'I said I would.'

'You might have changed your mind.' He looked her over. 'You look edible, Miss Logan. Your coat matches your hair.'

'Purchased by Kate last Christmas for just that reason,' she assured him, then raised an eyebrow as he led her back the way he'd come. 'Where are we going?'

'The tradesmen's entrance. Today's team are beavering away

in the Great Hall right now. So we'll sneak up to my place for coffee before I take you on the tour.' March led her through a tall, narrow door into a tall, narrow hall with stone walls and a lofty groined ceiling. He closed the door behind them and took Joanna's hands. 'Come with me to my lair, fair maiden. You can explore the rest of the house later.'

March took her past several doors and went ahead of her to a spiral staircase with stone treads worn smooth by centuries of use. He glanced at her suede boots. 'Sensible footgear. Good. This is where we climb.'

Glad to make use of the rope strung along the wall, Jo followed him up dizzying curves until they finally reached a door March opened with a touch of drama.

'Here we are.'

Jo stepped across the threshold into light. March's 'lair' was panelled, with windows on three sides giving a panoramic view of the gardens far below and acres of parkland and fields beyond them. 'How fabulous!'

March came up close behind her. 'So, what do you think?'

Jo looked round the room slowly. An open desk, overflowing with paperwork, stood in one corner, a huge oak cupboard in the other. Chintz-covered armchairs and a leather sofa sat in front of the big stone fireplace, grouped around a low table with newspapers, books and journals stacked alongside a coffee tray. A carved chest stood under one of the windows, an oval table covered in framed photographs under another. She smiled as she saw a pair of etchings on the panels between them, one of the gatehouse, the other the church.

'I said I'd show you my etchings one day,' said March, watching her.

Joanna's eyes widened as she recognised the signature. 'So, this is your "sort of flat".'

'Part of it. I'll show you the rest after we've had coffee. Help yourself to a cake and sit down.'

Joanna took a Chelsea bun from a silver basket and settled in a corner of the sofa. 'Yum, it's still warm. Is it something you made earlier?'

'No. I raided the tea shop. They're baked on the premises.' March filled the cups with steaming coffee from a jug, and added milk to hers. 'Is that to your taste, madam? I hear it's important to get the details right.'

'It's perfect,' she assured him, and smiled sheepishly as he took the opposite corner of the sofa. 'I was so nervous about coming here, March.'

His eyes glinted. 'In case I shut you up in my tower and had my wicked way with you?'

She shook her head, smiling. 'That never occurred to me.'

'I wish I could say the same! So, why were you nervous?'

'Stupid, I suppose. Maybe you bring women here all the time. But if you don't I thought the people who work here would be curious about me.'

'They are. But it's friendly curiosity. Though probably hopeful, too.'

'Hopeful?'

March shrugged. 'Some of them have known me all my life. They would like to see me with a wife and family.'

'But surely you must know dozens of females in your own—well…'

'Say *class* and I'll get angry,' he growled.

Jo scowled at him. 'I was going to say circle, set—whatever, Lord Arnborough.'

'Those of my acquaintance with the slightest appeal are either pursuing highly successful careers or already married to my friends,' he assured her. 'Have another bun.'

'Where are we having lunch?'

'Right here, after our tour, but I'm taking you out for dinner.'

'Am I staying for that, too?'

'Do you have something to rush home for?'

'Nothing until I cook lunch at Mill House tomorrow.'

March refilled their cups. 'So how is your mother?'

'Doing really well, thank goodness.'

'And the baby?'

'He's gorgeous. All's right with Jack's world since Kate survived Tom's arrival.' Jo smiled. 'As you've gathered, Jack thinks the sun rises and sets with her. And vice versa.'

'I witnessed the same phenomenon with my own parents.' March got up, holding out his hand. 'Right then, Miss Logan. Lord Arnborough is not in the habit of showing visitors over his home, but in this case he'll make an exception.'

'I'm honoured; but first I need to tidy up.'

'Then come to my bathroom, which I enjoy courtesy of Grandfather March's largesse.'

'Do we have to go back down those terrifying stairs to get to it?'

'No. There's a more modern, user-friendly version which leads to the main staircase. I brought you up the spiral to show off.' March led her across the room and slid a catch to open a section of the panelling onto a landing outside.

'How exciting—a concealed door,' said Jo rapturously.

'The three of us slept in the rooms along here,' March informed her, as they went down to the next floor. 'My room up there was once my mother's sitting room. In times past known as the solar. This is where I sleep now,' he added, showing her into a room with a plain, solid wardrobe and chest, a large matching bed, and very little else.

'You're very tidy!'

'Not really. I just stuffed everything in the wardrobe before you came,' he said, grinning. 'The bathroom's through that door in the corner. I'll leave you—'

'Don't go far,' she said, alarmed. 'I'll get lost.'

'I'll be waiting,' he promised, and trailed a finger down her cheek. 'Hurry up.'

When Jo rejoined him, her host was standing by the landing window, his profile outlined by the cold morning sunshine. She stood still for a second, thinking how perfectly he blended into his surroundings. As March said, he was what he was.

'Are you ready for the grand tour?' he asked, turning.

'Absolutely. Why else am I here?'

'To be with me, perhaps?' The sun struck glints from his eyes.

'That too,' she agreed demurely. 'So lead on, milord, where do we go first?'

'We'll do the main rooms before the punters arrive. So down to the Great Hall and the drawing room and so on, then we come back up to the first floor.'

Exploring Arnborough Hall with the owner was a lot different from looking over it alone. March had stories to tell about the artefacts, and fascinating snippets of provenance not mentioned in the guidebook. She already knew that the medieval part of the house, mainly the Great Hall, dated from the early fourteenth century, but not that March and his siblings had used it as a playground when they were young—something which Jo could picture so clearly it humanised the huge room and brought it to life.

'Not on open days, of course, but we used to have scooter races on rainy days in the school holidays,' March told her. 'Subsequent Arnboroughs have made additions through the centuries, but for obvious reasons money was short after the Civil War,' he went on, as they went on through the small drawing room and the grandeur of the dining room. 'The situation remained static until the Georgian Baron married an heiress. Fortunately Aurelia, the Regency bride, was passionate about maintenance rather than embellishment, except for the ballroom her nabob father insisted on, so otherwise the house is more or less as it was in the seventeenth century. My father's priority was to get the roof done.'

'The first time I came,' said Jo, as they entered the empty

ballroom, 'I imagined myself whirling around under these chandeliers in a gorgeous dress.'

'The next time I hire it out for a charity ball you can waltz with me,' said March.

'I'm not very good at that kind of thing,' she warned.

'You will be with me.'

Joanna smiled doubtfully. 'Where now? Portrait gallery?'

'The state bedrooms first.' March took her hand. 'We can boast of sleepovers for one king and two queens here—though not at the same time.'

'How impressive. I had to cut my original tour short before I got to the bedrooms.'

'Which was good. Otherwise we wouldn't have met again.' March looked down into her eyes for a long moment. 'We'll start with the King's Bedroom, where William of Orange once slept for a night—without Mary, his Queen.'

Joanna was enthralled as March led her from one room to another, each one with some special feature. Linen-fold panelling in one, in another an amazing plaster ceiling dating from the Tudor period and a fireplace with beautiful carving. But the most impressive things of all to Jo were a coronet and the crimson and ermine robes worn at the Queen's coronation.

'You're very quiet,' said March, as they reached the long gallery.

'I was thinking of the work it must take to look after all this.'

'My practical training comes in handy, and most of the people who help me have been working here for years. They're a good team.' He glanced down at her. 'Of course if I had someone to help me, as my father did, life would be a lot easier.'

'Can't you afford to hire someone?'

'I was talking about someone to share my life, Joanna. Not hired help.'

Joanna's eyes slid away. 'You must have a priest-hole?' she asked, to change the subject, then flushed at his mocking grin.

'In a Parliamentary household? Tut-tut, Joanna. Priest-holes are found in Catholic establishments.'

'Of course. Silly me.'

'Meet Aurelia—the heiress.' He led her to a portrait halfway along the gallery.

Jo gazed up at a young woman in a flimsy high-waisted dress, with dark hair in a knot at the crown of her head, and dangling ringlets escaping from it to soften a face the painter had failed to make beautiful. 'She had lovely eyes.'

'Plus a rich, social climbing father, who handed over a fortune as her dowry and gave the bridegroom a townhouse in Mayfair as a wedding present.' March looked up at the portrait with affection. 'Aurelia presented her husband with two sons and six daughters.'

'I hope she was happy.'

'Legend has it that she loved the Hall, so hopefully she was. If the weather keeps fine I'll show you her special garden later.' March went over to a window. 'Time up. The first of the visitors are here. Let's make a run for it.' He took her by the hand and hurried her along the gallery to whisk her through a door marked 'No Entry'.

'Do you ever get caught by people demanding information?' asked Jo breathlessly.

'If I do I plead ignorance and hand them over to a steward.' He glanced down at her. 'How do you feel about lunch?'

'Enthusiastic. Halfway through the tour I wished I'd eaten that other bun. I know now how little Tom feels when he's crying for his milk.'

'Is he keeping his mother up at nights?'

'And his father. They take it in turns with him.'

March shook his head in amazement. 'Your father is such a forceful personality it's hard to picture that.'

'Jack missed out on my early years, so he's making up for it with Kitty and Tom.'

'Of course! I'd forgotten you were adopted. Though to see you together it's hard to believe. He couldn't dote on you more if he were your biological father.'

'Actually, he is,' said Jo, smiling wryly as he stared at her in surprise. 'If you like, I'll tell you my little tale over lunch.'

'Oh, no. After hitting me so casually with that piece of news you expect me to wait?' March took her hand. 'Let's go back to the solar. Lunch can hang on for a while. Unless you're utterly famished?'

'No. Now I've started I may as well get on with it.'

Once they were back in the solar, March settled on the sofa beside Jo and took her hand. 'Right then, Scheherezade. Start your tale.'

'It's Kate and Jack's more than mine, which is why I asked permission.' Jo gazed into the logs laid ready in the fireplace. 'They fell madly in love when they were quite young. He was working in his father's building and contracting business, and on fire to expand it. But Kate was equally on fire to work in London, and she took it for granted Jack would find work there when she went, so they could be together. He flatly refused to do that, she flatly refused to stay, so they broke up and off she went.' Jo sighed. 'In London Kate not only pined desperately for Jack, she eventually found she was pregnant. She rushed back to tell him, only to hear that he'd married someone else just the previous weekend.'

March stared at her, dumbfounded. 'Good God! How did *that* happen?'

Jo flushed. 'Jack had missed Kate just as badly after she went—not least, being a mere male, the bed part. When he was pestered by a lady who, according to Kate, was sex on legs, Jack eventually succumbed. And then, being Jack, paid the price of a wedding ring when told that the lady was expecting his child.'

March swore softly. 'Go on.'

'Kate, utterly heartbroken at the news, went straight back to

London without contacting Jack. So he never knew she was pregnant. And Kate never heard that he'd divorced the bride who'd miscarried too far along into pregnancy for the child to be his.' Jo sighed, glad of his comforting grasp. 'In the meantime, Kate's married sister had begged to bring up the baby as hers, so I grew up in London thinking that my adored Kate was my aunt. Then when I was thirteen my adoptive parents—my real aunt and uncle—died on holiday in a car accident. I came to live with Kate in the house in Park Crescent and she met Jack again. Due to my resemblance to his mother, the truth came out.' Jo turned to him with a wry smile. 'The rest, as they say, is history.'

March shook his head in wonder. 'Small wonder your father feels protective, Joanna. He's missed out on half your life.'

'Far worse for Jack, he missed out on all those years with Kate,' said Jo soberly.

March slid an arm around her. 'The revelations must have been a hell of a lot for you to take on board at that age.'

'Oh, I was on cloud nine at first. I was a bridesmaid at their wedding; I'd gained a loving grandfather and a fabulous home. It was like a fairy tale, with Mill House the enchanted castle where we were all going to live happily ever after.' Jo smiled wryly. 'But all too soon the dreaded teenage hormones kicked in, and I began to change towards Jack. During school holidays at home he was so protective and strict with me I became resentful. Eventually I turned into a monster teenage rebel and even flung accusations at him, insisting that if he'd really loved Kate he would never have looked at another woman, let alone married one.'

'How did he take that?'

'Being Jack, he certainly didn't take it lying down. Kate was utterly appalled with me and flew to his defence, but he took the wind out of my sails by freely admitting his sins where the sexy Dawn was concerned.' Jo took in a deep breath. 'Then he looked me in the eye in that daunting way of his and told me I was wrong about the rest. He had never stopped loving my mother during all those lost years, he still did and always would. At which point Kate told me to go to my room and stay there until I could behave like a civilised human being. Not what I wanted to hear. I had expected Kate to take my side, and resented Jack even more when she didn't.' She shrugged. 'But something good came out of all that teenage angst. I worked like a demon to get into Oxford. But in retrospect it's pretty obvious I hooked up with Charlie there just to get at Jack.'

March's arm tightened. 'But your relationship with your father must have improved if you work together now.'

'It has. Though there were stormy scenes when I refused to go back to Oxford. But I knew very well that Jack loved my mother. Still does. He was so worried about this pregnancy he could hardly bear to let her out of his sight.'

'I can understand that. My father felt just the same about my mother. Which,' March added dryly, 'was fairly rare in the circles they moved in. It scotched any ideas that Lord Arnborough had married Miss Frances March for her money.'

'But she was so beautiful no one would have thought that anyway, would they?'

He shrugged. 'My father's shortage of cash was well documented. But, much against Randall March's wishes, his daughter chose a lowly baron in preference to the belted Earl dangling after her. She married for love and never regretted it.' March turned to look at Jo. 'Theirs was the perfect marriage.'

'Even though it caused your father so much grief when your mother died?'

'They had twenty-five years of happiness together first.'

She shivered. 'I'd rather settle for a nice, everyday kind of relationship, rather than a consuming passion which leaves you in pieces when it's gone.'

'Does your parents' relationship embarrass you, then?'

'Good heavens, no. At school I knew so many girls whose parents were divorced I thought it was romantic to have parents madly in love with each other. Though I've probably given you the wrong idea about Kate and Jack. They don't crawl all over each other in public, or whatever. It's just that having wasted so much time apart they spend every minute possible together.'

March eyed her closely. 'You say you resemble your grandmother, Joanna. Does that mean you look nothing at all like your mother?'

'The hair's the same, and we're built on the same lines, but that's it.' Jo smiled. 'Kitty's the spitting image of Jack, so I hope young Tom takes after his mama to even the balance.'

'You obviously love your little siblings. Would you like to have children of your own?'

'One day, maybe,' she said evasively.

March raised an eyebrow. 'You don't sound enthusiastic.'

'That awful endless day when Kate was in labour with Tom I got in such a state all my old resentment against Jack was revived and I cursed him for getting Kate pregnant again at her age.' Jo's chin lifted. 'I got over that the minute the baby arrived safely, but the experience rather damped down my personal desire to procreate just yet.' She smiled at him. 'And now I've embarrassed you quite horribly. I do apologise.'

March shook his head. 'Joanna, I'm the one who's sorry for bringing it up. But thank you for telling me your story. I was intrigued. Certain things about you didn't add up.'

'I know. That's why I asked permission to put you in the picture.' She smiled as they went downstairs. 'And after all that talking I'm hungry.'

'Good. Mrs Dean, my housekeeper, has left lunch ready for us in the dining room. But first I'll show you the kitchen.'

Daunted by the thought of lunch in that huge formal dining room, Jo eyed him in surprise. 'Surely she doesn't cook in that great cavern of a place I saw on the tour?'

'God, no. That's purely for show—to demonstrate the baronial lifestyle in times past. Mother turned the old scullery into a more viable kitchen during her makeover.' He smiled. 'I wanted to have this first time here alone with you, so I gave Mrs Dean the weekend off once she'd put everything ready this morning.'

Jo was relieved to hear it. She had not looked forward to scrutiny from Lord Arnborough's housekeeper.

The newer kitchen had once been the preparation area for the great baronial version adjoining it. Now it was a pleasant place, with bigger windows and modern appliances, and a huge scrubbed table with several unmatched chairs ranged round it.

'A bit bigger than my kitchen,' Jo commented.

'But nothing as *haute* as your type of *cuisine* ever comes out of it unless I'm entertaining,' March assured her. 'Mrs Dean is a good plain cook, and I'm grateful to her. But you, Miss Logan, are an exceptional—and beautiful—cook.'

Jo shot him a narrowed glance, but then flushed slightly as she saw he meant what he'd said. 'Thank you.'

'I never burn to make love to Mrs Dean, either,' he said casually, and led her through a door at the far end into a small dining room with a table laid for two. Its vaulted ceiling was a work of art, and the chairs grouped round the refectory table looked as though Oliver Cromwell had sat there at one time, but even so the effect was so much less intimidating than the grandeur of the state dining room Jo heaved a sigh of relief.

'What's wrong?' demanded March.

'Nothing.' She smiled ruefully. 'I thought we were eating in the other dining room.'

'With all the paying public passing through?' he said, laughing.

'So I was wrong,' she said crossly. 'I wasn't thinking straight. Your home tends to have that effect on me, Lord Arnborough.'

'Do *I* have the same kind of effect on you?' demanded March, pulling out one of the chairs for her.

'Certainly not,' she lied, though his throwaway line had taken her breath away. She watched as he filled two soup bowls from a pan sitting on the warming plate of a heated trolley. He put the bowls on the table, then reached into trolley for a basket of hot rolls and put it in front of Jo.

'*Voilá*!' he said, and sat down. 'Lunch is served. Mrs Dean wanted to put on a three-course meal and stay to serve it, but she can do that next time. Today I want you all to myself.'

Jo was in full agreement. She was all for getting used to March's way of life by degrees. Degrees? Did that mean she wanted to do this again?

'That's a strange look,' he commented. 'Don't worry. I promise you a proper meal this evening.'

'I wasn't worried. This soup is delicious,' she assured him. 'Are we going back to the Arnborough Arms tonight?'

'No. I've booked dinner at Easthope Court. It's a longish trip, but the food is worth it.'

'And now you've shed your disguise I needn't offer to go Dutch any more,' she said tartly, and eyed him uncertainly. 'But I'm not dressed for anywhere grand, March.'

'You look perfect just the way you are,' he said emphatically. 'More soup?'

'No, thanks. If we're going to Easthope Court I'll save myself for dinner.' To her embarrassment, Jo yawned a little as she put her spoon down. 'Sorry. It's the after effects of catharsis.'

March looked at her steadily. 'It was a privilege to hear your story, Joanna. Though it's hard to imagine you as a horrible teenager.'

She smiled ruefully. 'Believe me, I was.'

'If you say so. Would you like some coffee now, or shall we go straight back up to the solar and we can have some tea later? I'll light a fire, and you can put your feet up for an hour or two before we take off. It's a fair drive, so I booked an early meal. We'll leave about six.'

'I'm full of soup, so I'll go for tea later,' she said, getting up. 'You first. I need time for that spiral of yours.'

'Built to repel the enemy. But we'll take the kinder stairs this time.'

Once up in the solar again Jo felt warmer from sheer exercise. 'You need to be fit to live here,' she said breathlessly, 'no matter which stairs you use.'

'I am fit,' he assured her.

'I know.' Their eyes met.

'Right,' said March huskily. 'You wrap yourself up in that rug on the sofa until the room warms up, while I do what man has always done—provide fire for his woman.'

'That was only so she would cook for him,' retorted Jo, and gave a shout of laughter as he flipped a switch beside the cowled stone fireplace and ignited the deceptively authentic pile of logs in the fire basket into leaping flames. 'What a cheat! I thought the fire was real.'

He grinned. 'Did you really think I haul baskets of logs up those stairs?'

'Of course not. I thought someone hauled them up for you.'

'Parts of this house may date from the fourteenth century, but I live in the twenty-first, Joanna Logan,' he assured her. 'If you're cold, there's another electric heater in my bedroom.'

'No. I can feel the heat from the fire already. I don't even need the rug.'

'My sister Hetty's husband never ceases to marvel at life here. Cal is American, and his awe at the sheer age of the place is only outdone by his awe at its inconvenience.'

'Where do they live?'

'In LA, in a house with a pool and every convenience known to man. They also have a base here in this country—a house near the Thames at Sonning. But Hetty comes home to Arnborough regularly. Unlike Rufus, who does not,' added March, sobering.

'Does your brother live alone?'

He nodded. 'As I told you, Hetty took him to stay with Italian friends of hers after the accident. Now he rents a small house on the edge of a lake on their property. They have staff who see that he's fed, and Mario and Silvana get in touch if Rufus needs anything. Not that he does very often—other than more paint and canvas. And the money left to him by my grandfather more than covers that. So,' said March with emphasis, 'if you're still harbouring any guilt about him, believe me, Joanna, you don't have to. Rufus is leading his life in exactly the way he wants.'

'It's a relief to know that,' she admitted, and leaned her head back against the sofa cushions, smothering another yawn.

March sat down and put an arm round her. 'Lean on me and have a little snooze, if you like. I shan't complain if you snore.'

'I don't snore,' she said indignantly, then grinned. 'Or maybe I do, for all I know.'

'Relax, Joanna. Just close your eyes and float away for a while.'

'I can't do that,' she protested sleepily, but the leaping flames and March's warmth were too much for her. Against her will her eyelids drooped, and with a sigh she surrendered to sleep.

Jo woke to the rattle of teacups to find she was stretched out alone on the sofa under a rug, and shot up, eyeing March in dismay. 'I do apologise.' She glanced at her watch. 'Good heavens. Is that the time?'

'You've been out for the count for two hours,' he informed her, and handed her a cup of tea. 'Your life has been so hectic lately you obviously needed the rest, Joanna.'

'Bad manners in the circumstances,' she said, embarrassed.

'I'm flattered that you felt comfortable enough in my company to enjoy a little sleep,' he assured her.

'If you say so.' Jo sipped gratefully. 'This is nectar. Thank you, March.'

'My pleasure. And now you're awake I shall hand you today's paper to read while I get ready.' He bent down and dropped a kiss on her hair, then slid back the panel and went down to his quarters on the floor below.

Jo made no attempt to read. She finished her tea, then folded the rug and sat back on the sofa, her eyes on the authentic flames as she wondered about the woman March had asked to marry him. He had obviously been madly in love with the unknown Lavinia. The woman must have been plain mad to turn a man like March down. After all he was no pauper. He was also the most attractive man Jo had ever met in her life— not only physically, but in every way possible that a woman could want in a husband. If she wanted a husband—which she herself did not. Falling madly in love with a man did not equate with happiness. Something she knew only too well from her parents' experience. Kate and Jack were together now, but they'd travelled a thorny path apart before reaching their present state of bliss.

And love as a consuming passion was not for everyone. She could, Jo admitted, fall in love very easily with March Aubrey Clement. In fact, if she were honest, she already had. If only he wasn't part of all *this*! Jo got up restlessly and walked over to the windows to watch the light fading over the rolling green hills of Lord Arnborough's domain. She looked down on the formal lawns, where people were making for the gatehouse and the car park as the last of the visitors left, then turned abruptly away and went back to the sofa to stare into the flames again. March wanted a wife, and he was giving out signs that she qualified for the post. But he wasn't madly in love with her, as he had been with Lavinia. And, because she'd been kept in the dark about her true origins until she was in her teens, Jo had a tendency to be wary about all romantic relationships, let alone the kind March wanted.

She had one last dark secret she had not told March and never would. Nor anyone else. Even now she felt sick with shame at the memory of her jealousy when her parents had told her they were expecting a baby. Jo, at twenty-one, had been appalled at the prospect of sharing her mother with another child. But she had managed to hide it so well neither Kate nor Jack had suspected it. And when Kitty arrived the jealousy had changed to euphoric relief that her mother was safely through the birth. At first sight of her baby sister Jo had fallen so completely in love with Kitty it was impossible to believe, now, that she had ever been prey to jealousy. But a couple of years later the news that Kate was expecting another child at her age had filled Jo with emotion of a different kind. She had been furious with Jack—who had been well aware of it. Kate had been aware of it too, and had told Jo in no uncertain terms that it took two people to make a baby, which was the result of two people's love for each other, not a deliberate ploy to annoy their senior daughter.

Jo had come to terms with it mainly because Jack had not. He had been so frantic with worry about Kate right through the pregnancy that Jo had soon put aside her own qualms in her efforts to comfort him. Because, in spite of the stormy passages in their relationship, she loved her father very much. And calling him Dad for the first time had been a conscious effort to let him know that. Something Jack had been swift to understand and appreciate.

'You look deep in thought,' said March, startling her. 'Penny for them?'

Jo got up quickly, surveying his elegant suit and snowy shirt in admiration. 'Wow, don't you look gorgeous, Lord Arnborough?'

'I do my best,' he said modestly, and took her in his arms to kiss her so long and so hungrily her lips were swollen when he released her. He smiled into her startled eyes as he raised his head. 'I knew I wouldn't have a hope of that once you were ready.'

'You're right,' she said breathlessly, then looked down at her dress, relieved to see it had survived her nap remarkably well. 'Are you sure this will do?'

March gave her an all-encompassing scrutiny from head to toe. 'Oh yes. I'm sure.'

CHAPTER SEVEN

EASTHOPE COURT had once been the very grand home of a social-climbing Victorian industrialist. Now it was a privately owned hotel, recently refurbished to such splendour Jo wished she was wearing something more in keeping with her surroundings. Her dress fitted her to perfection, and it had been so expensive Kate had hidden the price tag, but it was nevertheless a black knit dress. Which would have looked a lot better with the new shoes she'd worn to Molly's, which had heels two inches higher than the black suede boots she was wearing.

Relieved of her coat in a ladies' room tricked out in Hollywood boudoir style, Jo touched up her lipstick, wished she'd worn more jewellery than just a watch and the plain gold studs in her ears, then, impatient with herself, went out into the foyer, where March was chatting with a man he introduced as the manager. The man personally led them through the palatial room, which was only half filled this early in the evening. He seated Jo at a window table, wished them a pleasant evening and left them to the care of a brace of waiters.

They were provided with huge menus, and their order was taken for wine, but Jo's eyes were riveted to the view of floodlit lawns and tree-fringed lake.

'Glitzy place,' she said, when they were alone.

March eyed her closely. 'You don't like it?'

She laughed. 'What's not to like? Fantastic view, and if the food lives up to the surroundings it should be wonderful.'

'It usually is. Though no better than the dinner we had at your friend Molly's restaurant.'

Jo smiled warmly. 'That's a kind thing to say.'

March touched a caressing finger over the back of her hand. 'It's the truth.'

Feeling the touch right down to her toes, Jo took refuge in her menu. 'What do you recommend?'

The dishes they ordered were exquisite to eat, and works of art to look at, but Jo's pleasure in the evening came to an emergency stop halfway through her main course when a husky female voice exclaimed, 'March! How lovely to see you.'

March rose to his feet as a blonde vision in sapphire-blue silk swept up to kiss him on both cheeks. 'Hello, Lavinia.'

The woman eyed Jo with interest and beamed at March. 'Aren't you going to introduce me, darling?'

'Of course.' He smiled down at Jo. 'Allow me to present Miss Joanna Logan. Joanna, meet an old friend of mine— Lavinia Fox-Hatton.'

'How do you do?' said Jo politely, with the warmest smile she could muster, and won a brilliant smile in return.

'So nice to meet you. A pity you've eaten already—we could have joined forces.' A slender arm adorned with a diamond bracelet waved imperiously. 'Over here, Jerry.'

A tall, heavily built man came strolling to join them. 'Hello, there,' he said, shaking hands with March. 'Haven't seen you in ages.' He smiled at Jo and gave her a graceful bow. 'Jeremy Fox-Hatton.'

After another introduction, and a few minutes' chat, he announced that he was ready for his dinner and took a noticeably reluctant Lavina away to a table on the far side of the room.

'Sorry about that,' said March when they were alone again.

'Why? Was it painful to meet up with the love of your life again?' said Jo tartly.

He shook his head, surprised. 'It's a long time since I thought of her like that, but, since you ask, it wasn't painful in the slightest. I meant I was sorry that our meal was interrupted. Won't you finish your dinner, Joanna?'

She looked at her half-empty plate and shook her head. 'No, thank you.'

'Then you must have a pudding.'

'I won't, if you don't mind.' Jo glanced at her watch. 'In fact, could we start back now? I have to drive home to my place after we reach Arnborough.'

'As you wish,' he said formally, and held up a hand to summon a waiter. 'I'll pay the bill while you get your coat.'

In case she met any more of Lord Arnborough's friends on the way out, Jo redid her face and hair in the powder room before she took her coat which the attendant brought. With a feeling of doom she braced herself as Lavinia rushed in.

'Off home this early?' she said, looking disappointed. 'I'd hoped we could all get together for coffee after dinner.'

Joanna smiled brightly. 'Sorry. Long drive home.'

Lavinia fiddled with her perfect blonde hair as she looked at Jo in the mirror. 'Have you known March long?'

'No. Not long.'

'Did he tell you he was engaged to me once?'

'Yes.'

'Seeing him again, I can't imagine how I brought myself to break it off. He was *so* in love with me, poor darling.'

'I know. He told me.'

'*Did* he?' Lavinia smiled like the cat who'd stolen the cream, then fixed Jo with a steely blue eye. 'Are you in love with him?'

'We're just good friends.' Jo smiled, doing her best to look coy. 'Forgive me, I must go. March can be so impatient. I hope we meet again,' she lied. 'Goodnight.'

As Jo hurried through the foyer a young man in hotel livery intercepted her, armed with a large umbrella.

'Miss Logan? Lord Arnborough is waiting outside in the car. Allow me.'

The journey home on the cross-country route was unpleasant. The rain was so heavy they drove through sheets of water in some places.

'You're very quiet,' said March after a while.

'I was afraid to distract you. It's not fun driving in these conditions.'

'Don't worry. I'll get you there safely.'

Jo had no doubt of that. It was the prospect of her own journey home afterwards that worried her.

'I met Lavinia again in the cloakroom,' she said, after a while.

'I know. I saw her go in. Did she upset you?'

'Of course not. Why would she do that?'

'God knows,' he said darkly. 'I thought she might be responsible for the *froideur* between us.'

'She did tell me you'd been very much in love with her.'

'But you knew that.'

'Yes. I told her so. She seemed very pleased.'

'It was a long time ago, Joanna. Lavinia has been married to Jerry Fox-Hatton and his millions for years.'

'How nice for her,' Jo said, in a tone which put an end to further conversation. Which, she assured herself, was just as well when the rising wind had begun snapping debris from the hedgerows to add extra hazard to the driving conditions.

'I should have brought the four-by-four,' said March, after swerving to avoid what looked like half a tree in the headlights.

'Afraid you'll hurt the car?'

'No,' he said through his teeth, 'I just want to get you home safely.'

But by 'home' March meant Arnborough Hall. When they arrived, Jo made for her car the moment he helped her out of his.

'I'll take off right away—' she began, but he seized her arm and ran with her towards the main door.

'Not in this,' he said flatly, and rushed her into the Great Hall which, despite its size felt like a haven of calm after the storm outside. All the lights were on, to Jo's surprise, and she experienced a surprising feeling of homecoming as she looked at the big, comfortable furniture which blended so well with the background of stone walls and ancient portraits, even with the suits of armour in their niches. She watched as March locked the doors, then smiled at him uncertainly.

'I'd better be on my way.'

'No. Stay the night. Please. You can't drive all that way in this.'

She glanced at the rain blowing in gusts against the windows, hating the very though of an hour's drive in this weather.

March looked at her steadily. 'There's no shortage of bedrooms. Will you stay?'

So he didn't expect her to share his, which took the pressure off. 'I want to,' she admitted, weakening at the persuasion in his eyes. Then a particularly wild gust hurled rain against the windows and made her mind up for her. 'That does it. Thank you. I'll take you up on your kind offer.'

'Excellent.' March took her hand to pull her to her feet. 'How do you feel about four-poster beds?' he asked as they went up the main staircase.

'I've never slept in one.'

'Now's your chance,' said March. At the other end of the landing from his bedroom he opened a door and switched on lamps to show her a room with similar windows to the solar, but here they were softened with damask curtains which matched the hangings round the bed and the skirt on the dressing table. A buttoned blue velvet chaise stood at the foot of the bed, with a vast double wardrobe and a bow-fronted dressing chest providing masculine notes of contrast in the feminine room.

'How lovely,' said Jo softly.

'This was my parents' room. Although my mother died in hospital, Father could never bear to sleep in here again,' said March. 'But he always kept the bed made up, and I've done the same.' As the words left his mouth a crack of thunder followed a lightning flash, and March grinned. 'Glad you agreed to stay?'

'Oh, yes,' she said thankfully, and looked round the beautiful room. 'Has anyone of note ever slept here?'

'Only my parents. And Hetty sometimes, on her own. She loves this room, but Cal's a bit long in the leg so they use Rufus' room, which has a bigger bed like mine. My grandparents used the King's Bedroom.'

Jo removed the damask silk cover and folded it carefully to leave on the chaise.

'No wonder your sister loves sleeping here.'

'Hetty will be delighted I've brought someone like you to sleep in it. Dinner invitations to the house in Sonning are fraught with danger because she usually invites some scary single female for me.'

'What do you do?' asked Jo curiously.

'I listen politely, make equally polite small talk, and make it clear I'm not on the lookout for a wife.'

She rolled her eyes. 'Surely they can't *all* want to marry you?'

March gave a snort of laughter. 'True. But one or two have hinted that dinner and a sleepover would do for starters.'

'And you never take up the offer?'

'No. I prefer to make my own choices.' He looked at her steadily. 'Where a wife and all other aspects of my life are concerned.'

'You lead a strange life in this great house of yours,' said Jo. 'You're Lord of the Manor, yet more self-sufficient than any single man I've ever met.'

'The shock of death duties tends to do that for one,' he said soberly. 'I had to find some way to keep this place. So economy, like charity, began at home. I do the land management side of things myself, and a surprising amount of revenue comes from letting the Hall out as a location. Also the dining room and ballroom are very popular for weddings—particularly in summer, when the garden is in full bloom. It's a photographer's paradise.' He smiled wryly. 'My father drew the line at weddings, but I live in the real world. As my practical sister said, if they do it at Blenheim Palace, why not at Arnborough Hall?'

'She's right. But the other thing you could do,' said Jo sweetly, 'is to follow in your father's footsteps and marry an heiress.'

'Like you?' he said swiftly, and gave her a look which set her hormones dancing. 'Rather than marry for money I'd prefer to wait until I find a wife willing to share this strange life I lead. One who cares for me enough to help with it.'

'So, instead of socialising with these importuning females your sister finds,' asked Jo, 'what do you do with yourself in the evenings?'

'I pop up to town and stay with friends sometimes. At home here I go over to the pub, catch up with paperwork, or even watch TV. Cal wanted to make me a present of one of those great flatscreen things, but even he had to admit defeat on that one. There's no place to put it. I keep mine in the oak cupboard by the fireplace.' March grinned. 'Cal's a really great guy, and oddly enough quite fond of me. I think the charm of my British eccentricity really gets to him.'

Jo had an idea that March Clement's charm probably got to most people he came in contact with—including the unimpressionable Molly and, that hardest of men to impress, her father. 'He sounds rather charming himself.'

'He is. Cal's no film star when it comes to looks, but he swept Hetty right off her feet just the same. He met her when he was checking out Arnborough for a film.'

'Did they get married here in your beautiful church?'

March chuckled. 'No, in Las Vegas.'

Jo rounded on him, grinning. 'You're joking!'

'I kid you not. Hetty was staying with a friend in Nevada, and Cal flew from California to meet her there. Like me, he believes in seizing the day. He railroaded her into saying yes, and then rushed her off to Las Vegas before she could change her mind.'

'Not in an Elvis chapel!'

'Unfortunately not. The ceremony was in some mock Victorian set-up Cal thought suitable for his English bride.' March smiled indulgently. 'But Hetty didn't feel quite married enough after that, so they came back here for a blessing in the church, and a reception for family and friends afterwards.'

'In the ballroom?'

'Yes. Though otherwise we do most of our entertaining in the Hall. Which is mainly when Hetty comes home. Cal spends Christmas here with us, instead of with his family, so I've solved that problem by asking the Sterns to join us for the past couple of years. It works well, because Cal takes Hetty home to California for Thanksgiving to even things out. Where do *you* spend Christmas, Joanna?'

'At Mill House, naturally. And this year I'll make sure I do everything possible to help Kate.'

'So you'll cook the turkey?'

'I'll do the entire meal. It's no hardship.'

'But you'll party a bit too?'

'Of course. I'll also babysit for Kate and Jack.'

March leaned against the bedpost, smiling. 'In short, you're a model daughter.'

'Now, maybe. But it wasn't always the case.' She flushed. 'I didn't mean to sound so Goody-Two-Shoes. It's just that my family means a lot to me.'

'Because you were late in getting together as a unit,' he said with understanding, and sighed. 'My family means a lot to me, too, but it's just Hetty and Cal these days. My parents were both only children, so I'm a bit short of relatives. And I'm damned if I can get Rufus to come home since Father died. I get over to the Parisis' place to see him when I can, but he's—I don't know—remote. He's been like that ever since—'

'I couldn't prevent my boyfriend from half killing him,' Jo finished for him.

March's eyes were suddenly stern as they bored into hers. 'Stop that, Joanna. You are not to blame. Nor will I allow it come between us. When I first saw you that day at the garden centre I thought you were married to the man with you, and I cursed fate for playing such a hellish trick on me. Then heaped blessings on it later, when I found you were single.' His mouth twisted. 'Tell me you felt at least something in return.'

'Oh I did,' she assured him. 'I told my mother I'd met this really hot gardener—'

'*What*?' March grinned, delighted. 'Is that true?'

'Oh, yes.' Jo looked up at him ruefully. 'I wish you still were.'

'I'm not hot any more?' he demanded, aggrieved.

She gave him a sharp dig in the ribs. 'I mean that I wish you were still just a gardener. But you're Lord Arnborough, and you live in this extraordinary place. While I'm just plain Joanna Logan.'

'Beautiful Joanna Logan,' he contradicted. 'And I believe we were meant for each other.'

To prove his point March lunged away from the bedpost to pull her into his arms. He kissed her hard and, having started, couldn't stop. When he raised his head at last they were both flushed and breathing raggedly, and he buried his face in Jo's hair, holding her close against his chest as though he would convince her by the hammering of his heart against hers.

CHAPTER EIGHT

THE room was very quiet for a long time as their breathing slowed. March took one arm away at last, but held Jo close in the crook of the other.

As though he thought she might run away if he slackened his grip, thought Jo. And smiled.

'What are you smiling at?' he asked huskily.

'My own arrogance.'

'Not a word I associate with you, Joanna. Explain.'

'I thought maybe you were holding me so tightly in case I ran off if you let me go.'

'You were right.' March smiled possessively. 'Though I'd catch you before you got very far.'

She looked him in the eye. 'Then I won't run.'

He breathed in deeply. 'So, Joanna Logan, have we finally managed to evict the elephant from the room?'

'Elephant?' Though she knew perfectly well what he meant.

'My title. It's such a huge obstacle for you it's dominating the space between us,' March said flatly. 'I may be the umpteenth Baron Arnborough, but I'm a perfectly ordinary bloke like anyone else.'

'A little less ordinary than some,' she retorted, and threw up her hands in surrender. 'All right. No more talk of titles.' She yawned suddenly. 'Sorry. I'm not bored, I promise—just a bit tired. It's been an eventful day.' She took her coat off and laid it over a chair, then sat down on the chaise.

'What do you normally do on a Saturday?'

'I usually go out with Isobel for a meal and a film, or a spot of clubbing sometimes. One or other of the twins tags along now and again. But last time Josh fell asleep in the taxi on the way back to the hospital, and it took Isobel and me, plus the taxi driver, to get him out.'

March grinned. 'Is he as hefty as the twin I met?'

'Carbon copy. In the struggle Isobel broke a nail or two, and I tore my dress. Luckily a hospital porter came to lend a hand, and we managed to load Josh onto a trolley. It was just exhaustion, poor thing. He'd only had one glass of wine.'

'You're very fond of him?'

'Very fond. And of Leo. But Isobel and I made a pact. Next time the twins want to socialise we meet up at her place or mine for a meal. If they fall asleep they can just stay put until they wake up.' Jo yawned again, and smiled ruefully. 'Sorry.'

March smiled. 'I'm selfish, keeping you talking instead of letting you get to bed.'

The words seemed to linger in the air. Jo tensed. The beautiful room, with only a pair of bedside lamps for light, seemed suddenly shadowy and mysterious, and an all too perfect setting for the love scene he probably felt she'd invited by agreeing to spend the night. This place was to blame. His enchanted castle was casting a spell on her. But she was no maiden in an ivory tower, waiting for a knight on a white charger to carry her off to a life of bliss. Attractive idea, though.

'It's early yet,' she said brightly, 'I wonder how things are at Mill House tonight? Jack's probably walking the floor with Master Tom as we speak.'

'I still find it so hard to picture that,' said March, shaking his head.

'Because my father's such an alpha male?'

'Probably. And I suppose I assumed a nanny would be looking after the baby at this stage. Sorry,' he added hastily. 'Absolutely none of my business.'

'Don't apologise. Jack was with you all the way on that, but Kate wouldn't hear of it. She's got Hazel in charge of the domestic side of things, which means she can look after the baby herself. She did the same with Kitty, too. *I* think it's because she was never able to do any of that for me,' added Jo, and changed the subject. 'Tell me about your childhood. It must have been wonderful growing up in a place like this.'

March smiled reminiscently. 'It was. For a long time parts of it were like a building site, which was paradise for Hetty and me—and for Rufus when he was old enough to trail round after us. My grandfather had settled a sufficiently large sum on my mother at the time of her marriage to finance some of the repairs and restoration necessary to turn Arnborough Hall into a viable family home. Far from being a spoilt beauty unwilling to lift a finger, my mother rolled up her sleeves straight after the honeymoon and helped her husband in every possible way. Our childhood was idyllic,' said March, a distant look in his eyes. 'But with hindsight I realise that my parents enlisted our help in countless small ways to make us part of things, to care for our inheritance. It seemed like play to us.' He sighed. 'Playtime ended for me the day I went away to school.'

'Eton?'

'Yes. How did you guess?'

'I met a few Etonians when I was up at Oxford. Were you homesick?'

'God, yes—at least at first. But I was good at sport, tall for my age, and full of the confidence my parents had nurtured in me. A bit cocky, really. I soon settled in. Some never did. God knows how Rufus survived.' March looked at her questioningly. 'How about you?'

'I went away to a school in the Cotswolds when I was eight.

But I loved it; I wasn't homesick in the slightest. It was Kate, unknown to me, who cried her eyes out alone in London because her baby had been sent away so young.' Jo shivered suddenly.

'You're cold?'

'Not really.'

'You just hate to think of your mother in distress,' he said softly.

'You're a very perceptive man.'

'Are you a perceptive woman?'

Her eyes widened on his. 'What should I be perceiving?'

'How much I want to kiss you again.' March pulled her to her feet and kissed her with such heat she melted against him. Her heart hammered against him as the kisses grew wilder and hungrier, until at last he raised his head a fraction, his eyes blazing with a look which took away what breath she had left.

'I want you so much, Joanna,' he said, in a rough, husky tone nothing like his usual drawl.

She nodded mutely.

'Do you want me?'

Jo nodded again, but with such reluctance March smiled wryly, and the tension between them lessened.

'But you have reservations?'

'Yes.'

He rolled his eyes. 'If the bloody title's the problem again—'

'No. It's not that. Please don't laugh.'

'Believe me,' he assured her, 'I'm not laughing. What should I not find amusing?'

'I'm probably taking too much for granted,' she said, hoping she wasn't making a huge mistake, 'and correct me if I'm wrong, but you appear to want more than just a session in bed.'

'Of course you're not wrong.' He arched an eyebrow. 'But why the hell did you think I would laugh?'

Her chin lifted. 'At my presumption.'

He grabbed her by the shoulders. 'God in heaven, woman,

you know damn well I want to be your friend *and* your lover. And one day a lot more than that,' he added, in a tone which left no doubt of his meaning.

'I'm up for the first two, March.' She braced herself. 'But if "a lot more" means something permanent, I'm just not the right one for you.'

His eyes bored into hers with an icy gold glare. 'You mean, Joanna, that I'm not the right one for *you*.'

Jo looked pointedly at March's hands until he removed them. 'No,' she said flatly. 'I don't mean that. I could very easily fall in love with you, but—'

The rest was lost as he kissed her with all-conquering triumph, taking her admission as licence to make love to her with an assurance she found hard to resist. Jo shivered as he stroked her breasts. Even through the wool of her dress their skilled, arousing touch caused fierce tumult as her sensitised nipples transmitted darts of sensation along every vein. The blood thundered in her ears, but when his hand slid to cup her bottom she stiffened, tearing her mouth from his as she pushed at his shoulders. She saw March change before her eyes from all-conquering lover to a man fighting for self-control.

He ran his hands through his hair, his face turned away. 'For God's sake, Joanna, I'm only human. How did you expect me to react to a statement like that?'

'I *thought* it might be my fault again,' she said bitterly. 'I would like to go to bed *here* now, please.'

'No need to be so precise,' he snapped. 'I know you didn't mean mine.' He turned to look at her. 'Why the devil did you tell me something like that?'

Her mouth tightened. 'It was a mistake, but it was the truth. It doesn't make any difference, March. The situation remains unchanged.' She halted suddenly, aware that a tide of embarrassed colour was rising in her face.

'Joanna,' he said, eyes softening, 'what's wrong?'

Her chin lifted. 'I may have confided my emotions, but you haven't said a word about yours!'

He gave a bark of mirthless laughter. 'Because I was afraid to frighten you away! Surely I've made my feelings obvious from the first day we met?' He glowered. 'Now, listen to me. Listen very carefully. Why do you think it was such a blow when I thought you were married?'

'You liked the look of me?'

He held her eyes. 'For me it was recognition. Something told me that in you I'd found a woman to share my life. I did the falling in love bit with Lavinia, but with you I felt I'd found a woman I could have a loving, solid relationship. With the kind to build a life on.' He took her hands, smiling sardonically. 'But you want to stay friends, maybe even make a perfectly natural progression to being lovers, but nothing more permanent than that. Which is a euphemism. In plain English you don't want to be my wife.'

Jo shook her head sadly. 'You're wrong there, March. I could get used to the idea all too easily. But then I would be Lady Arnborough, and that's just not for me.'

'Then it's checkmate.' He dropped her hands, smiling mirthlessly. 'Just my luck. The females Hetty pushes at me make it embarrassingly plain they'd jump at the chance to be my lady. Whereas the only lady I want declines the honour.'

When Jo also declined tea, and everything else he offered, March looked in a drawer in the chest.

'My sister keeps a few things here,' he said politely, and handed her a nightgown. 'Please make use of anything else you need in the morning.'

'How kind. Thank you.'

'Goodnight, then.'

'Goodnight.'

When the door closed, Jo hugged her arms across her chest, eyes tightly closed for a moment. Then, embarrassed by her own melodrama, she threw off her clothes and pulled the handful of lace and crêpe de Chine over her head. Her eyebrows rose as she caught sight of herself in the dressing table mirror on her way to the bathroom. A bit different from the night gear she normally wore, but it fitted so well Hetty had to be built on the same lines as her. At last Jo switched off the bedside lamps and got into bed, wondering if she was the biggest fool in the world for not jumping at March's proposal. After meeting Lavinia tonight she'd been as jealous as hell. Still was, purely because he'd been madly in love with the woman—whereas his emotions were far more stable where Joanna Logan was concerned. Did she *want* him to be madly in love with her, then? Of course she did.

Forget all that and go to sleep, she ordered herself. But, beautiful though the room was, in the dark it was scary. Overwhelmed by the centuries of antiquity surrounding her, she switched a lamp back on again for company, and settled herself against the banked pillows. March had made no mention of ghosts, but in a house this old there had to be at least one.

Along the landing March lay equally sleepless, for several reasons, not least of them the problem of unrelieved lust. Not that lust seemed the right word to associate with Joanna. For one wild moment earlier, when she'd actually admitted feelings for him, he'd thought Christmas had arrived early. Wrong. Whatever her feelings were, they did not equate with wanting to make love with him. He frowned. If he were just plain March Clement, who ran the estate and lived in a house like Ed Pargeter's, perhaps Joanna would have been in bed with him right now. Nothing he could do about that. There was no way he would renounce his title even if he could. He was the last of a long line of Clements. And if he didn't do something about it soon the line would end with him. Unless Rufus had a change of heart. Which was unlikely. He tossed and turned for a while, then swore when he realised he was so thirsty he'd never sleep without a drink.

To avoid waking Joanna, he got out of bed and into his dressing gown without turning on a light. On bare feet March stole along the landing in the dark, then let out a smothered howl as he stubbed his toe on a banister. The door of his mother's bedroom flew open.

'Who's there?' called Joanna sharply.

'It's just me,' said March, massaging his toe. 'Sorry I woke you.'

She stood in the doorway, watching him. 'I hadn't gone to sleep. Did you hurt yourself?'

'My fault for skulking around barefoot to get a drink. The idea was to avoid waking you. Would you like something?' He licked suddenly dry lips, wondering if she knew her body was silhouetted in detail by the light shining through the flimsy nightgown.

Jo knew. She stood her ground very deliberately to let him look. In the interval since they'd said goodnight she'd had a change of heart. Or body. This opportunity might never happen again. It was time to follow March's motto and seize the day. He might not be madly in love with her, as she was with him, but she wanted him to be her lover. Even if it was only for one night. But how to make that clear without literally throwing herself at him?

'I don't want a drink,' she said in sudden inspiration, 'but could you possibly keep me company for a little while? I found it a bit scary in the dark. It suddenly occurred to me that a house as ancient as this must surely have a resident ghost.'

'Of course it has,' said March, forgetting about a drink. 'Get back into bed and I'll tell you all about it.' He averted his eyes as she made for the bed, then followed her and sat on the edge of it once she was settled against the pillows. 'No clanking chains, or anything like that, just a lady who drifts along the long gallery searching, according to legend, for the lover who failed to turn up at the altar on their wedding day.'

'He developed cold feet?' asked Jo.

March shook his head. 'Killed by a rival suitor who lusted after Lady Blanche's dowry. Her father had always favoured the murdering rival, and married the unwilling Blanche off to him post-haste. Though it's generally held that she had the last laugh.'

'Why?' said Jo, fascinated.

'The son she bore was the image of the murdered swain.'

'You're making that up!'

March shook his head, wondering if Joanna had any idea how delicious she looked with her dark eyes like saucers. 'What's more,' he said, 'Blanche never bore her husband any children, so he was stuck with the other man's son as his heir.'

'Served him right,' crowed Jo. She bit her lip. 'Does Blanche keep to the long gallery, or does she wander further afield sometimes?'

'She's never been seen in this part of the house,' he said, with complete truth.

'Why doesn't that reassure me?' She slid down further under the covers. 'I really, really wish I hadn't asked about a ghost.'

'I could bunk down on the chaise to guard you from things that go bump in the night, if you like,' March suggested.

Jo thought about it, then nodded. 'But wouldn't it be horribly uncomfortable for you?'

'Not at all,' he lied manfully. 'I'd be far more uncomfortable in my own room, knowing you were lying awake in here, terrified that Blanche might join you.'

'Not terrified,' she protested. 'Just nervous.'

'I can't promise I won't snore, but at least you'll have company,' said March, enjoying the indecision on his guest's face.

'All right,' she said at last. 'And if the lady does come drifting in here you'll have to chase her out. After all, you're her descendant.'

'True. I'll just dash back to my room for my duvet.'

It was some time before March returned, and from his aura of soap and toothpaste it was obvious why.

'No sign of Blanche?' he asked, as he spread his duvet on the chaise.

'No.' Jo smiled at him from her nest of pillows. 'And now you're here I'm even brave enough to turn out the light.'

He moved to the side of the bed. 'You look very comfortable in there.'

'But you won't be on that chaise.'

'You could kiss me goodnight to make it up to me.' March leaned down, putting a hand on the bed either side of her. 'See? No hands.'

Jo laughed, and held up her mouth for the kiss he planted on it very fleetingly. But when he straightened she shook her head.

'Stay,' she whispered.

March's eyes smouldered into hers for an instant, then with a smile of triumph he slid into the bed to take her in his arms. For a while they lay completely motionless, then March ran a light, caressing hand down her spine and kissed the corner of her mouth. When the mouth smiled against his he locked his arms tighter and kissed her with all the pent-up passion he'd been fighting to control for what seemed like hours. With a gasp Jo's mouth opened, and his tongue surged to caress hers as he slid a hand beneath the lace covering her breasts.

'Wait,' said Jo. She pulled away to take the silk and lace over her head. 'If you're going to make love to me, I'd rather not wear your sister's nightgown!'

He gave a husky, delighted laugh. 'No *if* about it, my lady.' He planted kisses all over her face, one hand holding her against him as the other caressing hand paid loving attention to her taut breasts. At last his hungry mouth settled on hers with a heat and intensity that thrilled her to the core, his kisses demanding and receiving a response which tightened his embrace until every curve and plane of her body was locked against every angle and muscle of his. When his mouth left hers to follow a path down her throat, sucking on the pulse at the base, Jo's heart beat a frenzied rhythm. Her hips thrust against him in invitation which brought his erection seeking against her hot skin, and her breath caught in her throat.

'I won't hurt you,' he whispered, and continued on his downward path to close his mouth over her breast.

She gave a helpless moan at the sensation that was almost pain as his skilled lips and grazing teeth teased her nipples, arousing feelings so exquisite she let out a cry of protest when he stopped the torment. He held her fiercely close as he kissed her mouth again, his tongue surging in substitute penetration that drove them both wild. Without breaking the kiss he slid a caressing hand over her thighs, his long fingers moving on a tantalisingly slow voyage of discovery to learn how much she wanted him.

Jo herself had no idea just how much she wanted him until March found the little bud hidden beneath its hood, his skilled fingers arousing such extreme, piercing sensation she sank her teeth into his shoulder. With a fierce growl his body covered hers, iron-hard with the need to mate, his control suddenly gone as she dug her nails into his shoulders and reared up against him. With a visceral groan March slid home into hot, tight warmth which ripped his wits away. Her ragged gasp of pleasure was almost his undoing, but with teeth clenched he held her fast, his fingers gripping her hips to hold her still until he mastered himself enough to make love to her with all the skill at his command and bring them to the overwhelming climax they finally reached within seconds of each other.

It left them gasping for breath in each other's arms. And for March the discovery that a bridge had been crossed in their relationship filled him with elation.

He leaned out a hand and switched on a lamp, his eyes on Jo's face. He retrieved pillows from the floor to pile them up against the headboard and drew Joanna up to lean against them, then slid out of bed. 'I'll give you five minutes to yourself while I fetch a drink. What would you like?'

'Something cold, please,' she managed, breathless at the sight of so much muscular nudity.

March shrugged into his dressing gown and, aware of her discomfort, gave her a glinting smile on his way to the door. The moment it closed behind him Jo leapt out of bed and made for the bathroom. On the way back to bed she retrieved the nightgown and slid it over her head. She was propped against the pillow, the covers pulled well up, when March returned, armed with a bottle of champagne and a couple of flutes.

'Sorry I was so long. I went down to the kitchen for this,' he explained, filling the flutes. He handed one to Joanna and then got into bed with his own. He touched his glass to hers and smiled into her eyes. 'To you, and to the most glorious experience of my life, Joanna.'

'Glorious it was,' she agreed, ' but it doesn't change things, March.'

'Ah, but it does. Irrevocably. We are now both friends *and* lovers,' he informed her, with the confidence that was so much a part of him. 'It *is* possible to be both, Joanna.'

'You know this from experience?' she demanded, tasting her wine.

March leaned back against the stacked pillows, utterly relaxed. 'Only from observing my parents' marriage, and Hetty's. Personally I've known—still know—women who are just friends, and I've enjoyed encounters with others—including the mad, passionate interlude with Lavinia before harsh reality set in. But you are the one woman I want for life, Joanna.' He turned his penetrating gold gaze on her. 'Now you've given yourself to me, I'm keeping you. Get used to the idea.' He relieved her of the empty glass.

'March, be reasonable,' she protested, determined to set him straight. 'What or who you really need is someone who would be only too delighted to be Lady Arnborough. If we go on as lovers I would just get in the way.'

'The only Lady Arnborough I want is right here in my arms. So stop fighting your destiny, Joanna.' He drew her into his arms. 'This is where you belong.'

'That's not fair,' she protested, as he kissed her neck.

'A man must use all weapons to hand,' he said huskily, and removed the nightgown, his mouth and hands moving over her in such seductive persuasion that she was soon defeated by her own body. It responded to him with such fervour, and their climax engulfed them so convulsively, that at last tears slid from Jo's eyes as March held her in a bone-crushing embrace while the storm receded.

'Why are you crying?' he asked, kissing the tears away.

'I don't know. This is all so overwhelming, March. I've never felt like this before. The physical thing, I mean,' she added, sniffing inelegantly.

March rubbed his cheek against hers. 'Of course not,' he said with satisfaction. 'You belong to me.'

She eyed him askance. 'You sound so sure of that.'

'To put it another way,' he said, utterly serious, 'we belong to each other. And until death do us part. So, my darling, get used to the idea.'

CHAPTER NINE

UNACCUSTOMED to a man in her bed, Joanna woke early next morning. March didn't stir as she slid carefully to her feet. She gazed in silence for a moment at his sleeping face, then collected her belongings and stole along the landing to his bathroom to wash and dress as quietly as she could before going down to the kitchen. She switched more lights on for company while she made tea, and sat down to drink it, not sure whether last night had been the most wonderful experience of her life or the biggest mistake.

Eventually she made herself focus on the room. Could she really live here and preside over this as March's wife? Half of her shouted yes, yes, *yes*! But the other, more cerebral half, pointed out that mind-blowing sex was not, by a long way, the only skill required from the wife of Lord Arnborough. He needed a helpmeet, someone to share his life and responsibilities, as his mother had with his father. While she, unlike daughters brought up with their parents from birth, wanted more time to enjoy her relationship with Kate and Jack now it was on an even keel at last. And there was Kitty, and Grandpa. And now the baby, too. Also her much-loved house in Park Crescent to add to the mix.

The problem was, she thought despairingly, that she wanted March to be madly in love with her—the way he'd felt about the beautiful Lavinia. While he needed a sensible, capable wife to help him run Arnborough, and Joanna Logan filled the bill in the job description. But she just couldn't see herself as chatelaine of this ancient house with its centuries of history.

An hour went past unnoticed as Joanna drank cup after cup of tea and mulled over the problem. Suddenly she tensed at the sound of swearing as someone fought with the lock on the kitchen door, and then a man burst into the room to dump down a pile of luggage. A thin, haggard stranger with a mane of shaggy fair hair stared at her in shock. Then his eyes lit up in wonder and he shot across the room to yank her to her feet, scaring her out of her wits.

'Jo Logan? My God, is it really you—?'

'Yes, it is,' said a harsh voice, and March erupted into the kitchen to pull Jo away. 'Where the hell have you sprung from, Rufus?'

But his brother was too focussed on Jo's face to answer. 'It's a miracle.' He turned to March with a smile of blazing gratitude. 'She really is alive—you found her.'

'I found her, yes,' said March grimly. 'But not for you. She's mine.'

'What?' Rufus pushed the hair back from his face, his blue eyes blank with incomprehension. 'What the hell are you talking about?'

'We met by chance right here at Arnborough,' March informed him. 'Nothing to do with you, old fellow.'

Joanna detached herself from his possessive grasp. 'Your brother is right, Red. Sorry—Rufus. He thought Joe Logan was a man. We'd known each other for a while before he discovered my connection with your accident. I'm so deeply sorry about that,' she added. 'I hope you're fully recovered.'

'Yes, thanks. But never mind that,' he said impatiently, and glared at his brother. 'Why the hell would you think Jo was a man?'

March glared back. 'There was no mention of gender in your ravings. It was a simple mistake.'

'Which you probably didn't even bother to follow up!'

March controlled himself with effort. 'You know damn well I did, Rufus. So did Father, and the police. But there was no evidence that anyone other than you and your friend Peel had been in the car. I'm telling you the truth. I met Jo for the first time quite recently, right here, at the garden centre.'

Rufus stared dully from Jo to his brother, then rubbed his eyes like a weary child, his face ashen. 'God-awful headache,' he muttered. 'Sorry. I feel a bit…' He sagged. March leapt to catch him, and propped him on the nearest chair.

'Heavens, March, he looks ghastly,' said Joanna in alarm, and felt Rufus's pulse. 'You'd better call a doctor.'

'First I need to get him upstairs.'

'Right. I'll help you carry him. Is the bed made in his room?'

'Probably not. I'll put him in mine for now.' He looked at her closely. 'Apart from all the drama, how are you today?'

'Shell-shocked,' she said tersely, feeling her colour rise as she met his eyes.

'As a result of last night?' he whispered.

'Yes. And now this,' she added, gesturing at the unconscious face of his brother. 'I'd better help you get him upstairs before I go.'

'Go?' March frowned.

'I'm on kitchen duty at Mill House today, remember.'

'Oh, God, so you are. But after we get Rufus in bed we talk before you take off,' he warned.

'We certainly will,' she said ominously. 'Grab him by the shoulders and I'll take his feet.'

But March simply heaved his brother up and over his shoulder in a fireman's lift. 'Up we go,' he said breathlessly.

'For God's sake be careful,' Jo implored, following behind.

'Don't—worry—I won't—drop him.'

'I'm more afraid you'll do damage to yourself!' she retorted, and mounted the stairs behind March as he bore his brother at a steady pace up the stairs to the landing, then let him slide to his feet, keeping a tight hold of him while he took a breather.

'There's not much flesh on him,' he panted, 'but he's heavier than he looks.'

'Are you all right?' demanded Jo.

'I will be once baby brother's safe in bed and I've rung a doctor.' He heaved Rufus up again, cursing under his breath as his phone rang in his back pocket. 'Fish it out and see who it is, darling, will you?'

Jo eyed the caller ID with misgiving. 'It's your sister.'

'Answer it, then.'

'Hello?' she said reluctantly.

'Hi, Henrietta Stern here. Is my brother there?'

'Just a moment. I'll get him for you.'

Once Rufus was safe on the bed, March took the phone from Jo. He flung an arm round her waist and held her close as he spoke to his sister, who was apparently arriving home that afternoon.

'That's bit of a surprise, Hetty, I thought you were coming next week. Just as well, though, because Rufus turned up just now, looking the worse for wear. He needs a doctor. But I *was* able to introduce him to Miss Joanna Logan, the lady who spent the night here with me.' He laughed. 'Yes, she is. I'll fill you in when you arrive. See you.'

March took Joanna by the hand and led her outside to the landing. 'I know you want to hit me, but hang on while I find out who's on call.' When he got through to the medical centre to describe the problem a call was promised within minutes, but Jo glared at him as he put the phone back in his pocket.

'Why on earth did you tell your sister that? She'll assume I'm your lover.'

'Because, my darling, that's exactly what you are.' He took

her in his arms and kissed her protests into silence. 'At least,' he added, 'until you agree to be a whole lot more than that.'

'Which I won't,' she said, when she could speak.

March smiled indulgently. 'Of course you will. As I've said before—get used to the idea.' He took her hand and led her back to his room, to find Rufus staring up at them blankly.

'What happened, March?' he asked hoarsely. 'How did I get up here?'

'You passed out. I carried you up.'

Dazed blue eyes turned on Joanna. 'So you *are* here, Jo. I didn't dream it.'

'No,' she agreed. 'How are you feeling, Rufus?'

'Pretty awful.' The eyes narrowed. 'Are you going to marry March?'

'No, I'm not—'

'Yes, she is,' said his brother with emphasis.

Jo glared at him, then glanced at her watch. 'I must be off soon, but I can make you some tea first, Rufus, and something to eat.'

He shuddered. 'No, thanks. Head aching too much. Feel sick. Where are you going?'

'Home—to cook lunch for my parents.'

This seemed to be more than he could take in. With a weary sigh he closed his eyes.

March eyed his pallor with misgiving. 'Just rest for a bit, Rufus, until the doctor comes.' He led Jo from the room. 'Do you have to go?'

'I should,' she said, torn, then sighed, resigned. 'All right. If you'll give me your phone I'll see if I can arrange things so I can stay for a while to help.'

March's eyes lit with such gratitude she almost forgave him. 'But only if it doesn't inconvenience your family.'

'It won't.' Jo pressed a few buttons. 'Hi, Molly, it's Jo. I hope you weren't still in bed. Can you do me a big favour?'

While she was talking the doctor arrived. After a hurried

consultation March touched a hand to Jo's shoulder and led the doctor off to examine the invalid. Once Molly had promised to deliver Sunday lunch for the Logan family promptly at one, Jo rang her mother to explain the situation. 'The thing is, March desperately needs a helping hand. The doctor's with his brother right now, but I'd like to stay for a bit. I've organised lunch for you. Molly's sending it over. My treat.'

'*Joanna!* There was no need to do that.'

'Yes, there was. Otherwise Hazel won't take the day off. Apologise to the others, and tell Kitty I'll see her tomorrow on my way home from work.'

'All right, darling. By the way, if you stayed overnight, where exactly did you sleep?' asked Kate sweetly.

'In the fabulous room once occupied by March's parents. You'd love it. Look, must dash. See you tomorrow.'

Jo snapped March's phone shut, smiling anxiously as March introduced her to the doctor as 'a friend of the family'.

'Rufus is battling with one of the severe migraines he's been subject to since his accident some years ago,' said the doctor, his eyes alert as Jo winced. 'Are you all right, my dear?'

'My brother's collapse gave her a scare,' said March, putting a possessive arm round her.

'Hardly surprising. I've given him an injection, so he should sleep for several hours. When he wakes he'll feel better, so give him plenty of fluids and try to make him eat something light— soup or eggs.' He shook March's hand. 'Don't hesitate to call me if you need me. Rufus told me he's brought his prescription medication with him, but if he needs more contact the health centre.'

March saw the doctor out, then returned to Jo. 'Can you stay?'

She nodded. 'Molly's sending lunch over to Mill House, and I've rung my mother to explain. Kate's curious, to say the least.'

'Because you stayed the night?'

'More because I'm staying for the day.' She eyed him wryly. 'Now I suppose I've got to face your sister too.'

'Thank you, Joanna. It means a lot to have you here with me.'

'Then I'll make myself useful and rustle up some break-fast.' She relented suddenly, and smiled up at him. 'How about a fry-up?'

'First I need this.' March bent his head to kiss her, then held her close against him, rubbing his cheek against hers. 'I'll take Rufus's things upstairs and check on him. Then I intend, come what may, to concentrate on the pleasure of my first breakfast with my future wife. But,' he added, his eyes holding hers, 'only the first of many.'

'Are you going to keep saying things like that to indoctrinate me?' she said, scowling at him.

'I hadn't thought of it that way, but it's a good plan!' He picked up the scruffy selection of baggage and sent her a searing look as he went from the room.

Jo watched him go, wondering why the tall, rangy figure in an ordinary navy jersey and jeans was so much everything she'd ever wanted in a man—except for the title and the daunting splendour of his home. She sighed, ran an assessing eye over the cooker, and got to work.

By the time March came back she'd set the table, a platter of crisp grilled bacon was in the warming oven, and she was about to break eggs into the frying pan.

'Perfect timing,' she said, smiling. 'How is he?'

'Sleeping like the dead. I'm glad I got his clothes off while the doctor was here. Rufus is so out of it now I wouldn't have a hope of undressing him,' he told her. 'Apparently oblivion for a few hours is the best thing for him. It was sheer luck Dr Harwood was on call. He saw Rufus through his convalescence after the accident. He was also a huge support to me during my father's final illness.' His eyes narrowed. 'When my brother does wake up I'll have some questions to ask.'

'Just concentrate on breakfast right now. How about making some toast while I finish the eggs?' suggested Jo.

March set to work. When he set the filled toast rack on the table he drew in a deep breath of pure satisfaction as Jo set a filled plate in front of him. 'Perfect. All Sundays should start like this—minus the early-morning drama.'

Jo sat down to her own meal, suddenly famished, then flushed when it dawned on her why.

'What were you thinking about just then?' asked March, reaching out a hand to touch hers. 'Something to do with last night?'

'Yes,' she muttered, buttering toast feverishly. 'I hadn't realized—'

'Realised what, my darling?'

'That one felt so hungry afterwards.'

March gave a delighted laugh. 'None of your other essays into romance had the same effect?'

'Heavens, no. And I'd hardly describe them as romance. Besides—' She stopped dead.

'Besides?' he prompted.

'It was so different with you,' she muttered.

'I should hope so!' His fingers tightened. 'Tell me how.'

'You made love to me more than once. I thought that only happened in books.'

March speared her with the direct look she was getting to know so well. 'Did you spend the night with the others?'

'No. Never.'

'That explains it. If a man holds a girl in his arms all night he's bound to wake and want to make love to her—if only first thing in the morning.' He gave her an accusing look. 'Which would have happened *this* morning, but the bird had flown. Why?'

'I woke early and just had to get up. You were fast asleep, so I tried not to disturb you.'

March's eyes narrowed. 'Did you have some idea of taking off for home before I got up?'

'No, of course not,' she said indignantly. 'I came down to the kitchen to make tea and do some thinking.'

He relaxed slightly, and helped himself to more toast. 'Did I feature in your thoughts?'

'Of course you did—until your brother burst in and scared the living daylights out of me. I didn't recognise him, March.'

'I'm not surprised. He looks terrible. You'd think that someone living in sunny Italy by a lake would look a damn sight better than Rufus.' He frowned. 'I still have no idea why he's here. Hetty doesn't either. But she soon will. She's better at dealing with him than I am.' He looked at his watch. 'I'd better ring Mario—let him know Rufus has arrived.'

'I'll clear this lot away, then make some coffee while you're doing that.'

March smiled at her as he got up. 'This is so good, Joanna.'

She didn't pretend to misunderstand. 'Nevertheless, I'm not weakening,' she said firmly as she got to her feet.

His smile widened. 'Aren't you? I'll just go upstairs and use a landline for the call. I'll have a look at Rufus on the way down, then enjoy my coffee with you in peace.' He dropped a kiss on her hair on his way past, and strode from the room.

By the time March came back Jo had cleared away all signs of breakfast. 'Did you find out anything?' she demanded.

'No. Apparently Silvana and Mario are away, but my Italian isn't good enough to understand the housekeeper too well.' March pulled her into his arms. 'Rufus is still out for the count.'

Jo leaned against him for a moment, needing the contact. 'So let's sit and enjoy our coffee. By the way, is your sister staying tonight?'

'Forgot to ask. Why?'

Jo eyed him in exasperation. 'If she is, presumably she will need dinner. So will you. And Rufus, too, if he's up to it.'

March planted a hard kiss on her lips. 'I do so love a bossy woman. Correction. I love *my* bossy woman. But let's have that coffee before we let the rest of the world intrude. Which reminds me,' he added as Jo filled coffee mugs. 'How the hell did Rufus get here so early?'

'No idea. Taxi?'

'It would have to be. There's no train at that hour.' March tasted his coffee. 'That's wonderful. It never tastes like this when I make it. The magic ingredient is obviously your company while I drink it.'

'Thank you, kind sir! Do you want me to cook lunch when Hetty arrives?'

'Certainly not. We'll eat at the pub.'

'Then I'd better give the redoubtable Trish a ring and organise it. Or better still take a stroll over there while you have a shower. I need some fresh air.' And some time on her own...

March seized her in his arms and kissed her. 'You may do whatever you like, my darling. And no more nonsense about the role of Lady Arnborough. You were born to play it.'

'Oh, I probably could *play* it well enough for a while,' she admitted. 'But living it on a permanent basis is a different thing altogether.'

CHAPTER TEN

AFTER a leave taking from March which left her flushed and breathless, Jo walked briskly to the pub.

'Good morning.' She smiled when Dan opened the side door in response to her knock. 'I decided to pop over rather than ring. Could I have a word with your wife about a meal?'

'Of course, Miss Logan.' He ushered her into the kitchen. 'Young Rufus turning up out of the blue was a surprise. His brother had no idea he was coming?'

'No.' Jo smiled as Trish came in. 'Hello, I need assistance.'

'What can we do for you?' said the woman instantly.

Jo explained the situation. 'I'm not sure what time Mrs Stern is arriving, but could you provide lunch when she does?'

'Of course. Just give me a ring later.'

Jo thanked her warmly, then frowned. 'It's just occurred to me—how did you know Rufus was here?'

'The friend who drove him here had booked in for both of them,' Dan told her.

Trish nodded, looking worried. 'But Rufus was up with the lark this morning, and no matter how I coaxed I couldn't get him to eat breakfast. He looked so poorly I was worried.'

'Migraine,' Jo explained. 'It was so bad Dr Harwood gave Rufus an injection to help him sleep it off. Did you know his friend?'

Dan shook his head. 'Never seen him before last night. Nice motor, though. You'll probably bump into him on the way back. He went for a walk.'

Jo thanked them both, but refused offers of coffee. 'I'd better get back.'

On her way back to the Hall, she stiffened as she saw an all too familiar figure leaning against the sundial in the middle of the terrace. At the sound of her footsteps the man turned, then smiled, his eyes widening in astonishment.

'*Jo*! What are *you* doing here?'

She eyed him coldly. 'I might say the same of you, Charlie. I hear you drove Rufus to the Arnborough Arms last night. Where from?'

'Heathrow.' He seized her hand. 'How are you? Not that I need ask. You look wonderful. I suppose you've come to look over Arnborough Hall? Amazing place. But it's early yet. Let's catch up over a drink at the pub.'

'No, thanks.' She pulled her hand away, and smiled as March came sprinting to join her. 'All sorted with Trish.'

'Good. I was wondering where you'd got to.' He turned to the man watching them in astonished silence, and instantly morphed into Lord Arnborough. 'Why, Mr Peel,' he said coldly. 'What are you doing here?'

'He drove Rufus here from Heathrow last night,' Jo informed him. 'They stayed overnight at the Arnborough Arms.'

Charlie quailed visibly at the look on March's face. 'It's all right. I've got my licence back.'

'How reassuring,' said March affably. 'I salute Rufus for his bravery.'

Charlie flushed. 'Is he around?' he added hopefully. 'He said he'd give me the tour before the punters arrive.'

'I'm afraid there's no chance of that,' March informed him curtly. 'My brother collapsed earlier, with one of the blinding migraines he's been subject to since the accident. Our doctor gave him an injection and he'll sleep for hours yet. Now, if you'll excuse us, we have things to do. When Rufus wakes I'll tell him you called.'

'Thank you.' Charlie turned away, crestfallen, then paused, eyeing Jo blankly. 'But where do *you* fit into all this? You hardly knew Red.'

March took Jo's hand. 'Joanna is staying here as my guest.'

'He was speechless,' said March with satisfaction. 'Though I intend to have a word in my brother's ear. He must have been mad to get in a car with him again.'

'Charlie's changed a lot. He looks so much older it took me a minute to place him.'

'When did you last see him?'

'I haven't laid eyes on him since the night of the accident. We had such a struggle when I tried to take his car keys away I lost my balance and fell over. By the time I was on my feet again Charlie was driving off. I wasn't hurt,' she added hastily. 'Right. Let's check on Rufus, then have some more coffee.'

'Perhaps you could make a start on that,' said March casually, 'while I go over to the pub for a word with Dan.'

Jo stiffened. 'And a word with Charlie at the same time?'

'Yes,' he said baldly.

'Please don't.'

His mouth tightened. 'You don't want me to hurt him?'

'Not on my account.' Her eyes held his. 'If you do want me to get used to the idea of marrying you one day, Lord Arnborough—'

'You know the answer to that!'

'Then cut back on the testosterone and engage your brain. Think of the fuss a fight with Charlie would cause on your own doorstep if it involves me.'

His fists unclenched. 'You're right, blast it. Hell of a pity, though. I'd give a lot to rearrange his face.'

'I rather think,' said Jo dryly, 'that Charlie knew that.'

'He'd better stay the hell away from Rufus,' said March as they went upstairs. 'Why do you think he got in touch with him? To apologise?'

'If he did it was a means to an end—an entrée into your world. Charlie's a climber. I was too young to realise my main attraction for him was my relationship to Jack.' Jo pulled a face. 'I didn't have much else going for me, because according to Charlie I didn't know how to please a man. Not sexy enough.'

March seized her by the hand and hurried her along to his mother's room. 'Stay here for a moment,' he ordered. 'I'll just take a look at Rufus.'

Jo gazed down at the rumpled bed, suddenly warm at the memory of the rapture she'd experienced in it. March had shown her beyond all doubt that she'd pleased him in every possible way.

'He's sleeping peacefully,' March reported, and took her in his arms. 'Joanna, there's something you should know.'

She looked up at him with misgiving. 'You've got a wife locked up in a tower somewhere?'

'No. Nothing so melodramatic. I'd met Charles Peel only once before today, when he was in floods of tears over Rufus. I had my suspicions then, but seeing him again today confirmed them. You had no hope of pleasing him in bed, my darling, because, although he may still be lurking in the closet, he prefers his own sex.'

Jo stared at him. 'Is Rufus—?'

'Lord, no. His fey kind of looks probably appeal to Charlie no end, but the only woman who's ever interested Rufus is you.' March's mouth tightened. 'But you're mine.' He kissed her hard, by way of emphasis, and Jo responded with a joyous agreement which delighted March so much he raised his head a fraction, his eyes gleaming into hers. 'Let's have a nap.'

Jo blinked. 'Surely you don't mean—?'

'I most certainly do,' said March, and began undressing her at speed, kissing the places he laid bare with such demand they surged together with no preliminaries other than their need for each other, surrendering to the relentless rhythm that brought them at top speed to the fierce, throbbing rapture of fulfilment.

'Convinced now that you're sexy enough?' said March roughly.

'Getting there.' Jo smiled at him. 'Though I may need further convincing some time. But not right now. If I can trust my legs to hold me up I'd better do something about this bed while you check on Rufus. Will Hetty want to sleep in here?'

'No. I will. She can keep to Rufus's room, as usual.'

'Then I'll leave you to tidy the bed, milord. I'd like a bath. Have I got time before your sister arrives?'

'Of course you have. It's just my kid sister,' he reminded her. 'Not a state visit.'

Jo felt so much better after the fastest bath of her life she no longer had qualms about meeting the Honourable Henrietta Stern—who, Jo had discovered, had very provocative taste in underwear.

'Shall I confess to Hetty that I borrowed some of her things? They're a lot saucier—and pricier—than mine,' she said, when March came back to report that Rufus was still sleeping peacefully.

'Confess if you want to. But I doubt she'll miss them. Cal buys her that kind of stuff all the time, apparently.' He grinned. 'I'll do the same for you once we're married.'

'Stop that!' she said irritably. 'Doing the lord and master bit won't work, March Clement.'

'I'm not that bad,' he protested.

'No, you're not. Quite the reverse. I thought you were hot the first time we met,' she reminded him. 'And recently, Lord Arnborough, you've given me indisputable proof that I was right.' She flung out her arms to keep him off. 'No, you don't.'

March took no notice. 'You can't say things like that and

expect me to stay tame, Joanna Logan,' he said, hugging her. 'Thank you for the compliment. A man likes to know he's come up to scratch as a lover.'

'A woman does, too!'

'You can't still have any doubts?' He rubbed his cheek against hers.

'My confidence in my charms was squashed early on in my career.'

'Damn Charlie Peel to hell,' said March savagely, and kissed her until her head reeled. 'You are everything a man could want. Intelligent, capable, beautiful, a damned good cook—and as icing on the cake you're also dynamite in bed.'

But it wasn't enough. Because she wanted him to be passionately *in* love with her—the same way her father felt about Kate. Tears of disappointment welled in her eyes.

March kissed them away, mistaking the reason for them, then went off to check on Rufus. When he came back he looked worried.

'He's so utterly still, Joanna. He's breathing regularly, and his pulse is all right, but should he be sleeping this long?'

'If you're worried, ring the doctor again.'

'I'll leave it for an hour or two; then if he's still the same I will.' He held out his arms. 'Now, come and comfort me. I just want to hold you for a while.'

'Put that woman down, March Clement, and give *me* a hug,' ordered a laughing feminine voice, and March released a hectically flushed Joanna to greet the woman smiling in the open doorway.

CHAPTER ELEVEN

ON HETTY STERN her brother's dark good looks were translated into beauty so vivacious her smile was irresistible. Her black hair hung straight and glossy to the shoulders of a fringed suede jacket worn with jeans and cowboy boots, and great gold hoops swung in her ears as she launched herself at March for her hug.

She planted smacking kisses on his cheeks, then shook him slightly. 'Come on, then. Introduce me.'

March's lips twitched as he caught Jo by the hand. 'Joanna—meet my sister, Mrs Calvin Stern. Hetty—allow me to present Miss Joanna Logan.'

Hetty's sharp eyes looked from his face to Jo's. 'Am I jumping the gun to offer congratulations?'

'Afraid so,' said March. 'I want her to marry me, but she needs persuading.'

Hetty took Jo by the hand. 'You don't like him enough?'

Jo flushed. 'That's not the problem -'

'She would much rather I was plain March Clement,' he explained for her.

'Do you love him, Joanna?'

March's eyes lit up as Jo nodded, flushing. 'Yes, I do.'

'Then what does his title matter?'

'It's not *his* title I worry about. I just can't see myself as Lady Arnborough,' sighed Jo.

Hetty laughed and patted Jo's hand encouragingly. 'You'll get used to it. You certainly look the part. You're gorgeous.'

'So are you,' said Jo sincerely.

'Thanks! You like the gear? Rodeo Drive meets Calamity Jane. I'd murder a cup of tea, by the way, but first I'll just pop up and see baby brother.'

'Leave that until later. He's sleeping right now. And we can do better than just tea, Jo has arranged lunch.' March filled a kettle while Jo set the table with a light lunch of poached salmon.

'Fill me in, then,' said Hetty, sitting down at the table. 'What brought Rufus home?'

'No idea.' March supplied Hetty with what details they knew, including the doctor's visit.

'You mean Rufus actually let Charlie Peel drive him here?' Hetty rolled her eyes. 'Idiot. No wonder he's got a headache. How did *that* come about?'

'I don't know yet.'

'What March hasn't told you,' said Jo, deciding to get it over with, 'is that I'm the Jo Logan Rufus was so worried about after his accident. I was up at Oxford at the same time. Charlie Peel was my boyfriend.'

'Joanna tried to take his car keys away that night, but he fought her off,' said March grimly.

'The swine!' Hetty's huge gold eyes opened in wonder. 'But how amazing that Jo Logan was a girl all the time. And how clever of you to track her down at last, March.'

'Actually, I didn't.' March reached to touch Jo's hand. 'Fate did it for me. We met right here—at the garden centre. Joanna was buying plants for her mother.'

'I thought he was one of the gardeners,' explained Jo.

'While I thought she was married.' March helped himself to more salmon. 'I was deeply depressed about that, until I met up with her later and found she was single.'

'I was with my father and my little sister,' explained Jo.

'How marvellous,' said Hetty, rapt, and smiled at her brother. 'So you fancied her like mad right away?'

'Yes,' he said simply, and smiled at Jo.

'How about you, Joanna?' demanded Hetty.

'It was pretty much the same for me,' admitted Jo. 'I even told my mother I'd met this really hot gardener.' She shot a dark look at March. 'But he was pretty secretive about himself. We'd known each other quite a while before I found out he was Lord Arnborough.'

'She was mad as hell with me.' March grinned evilly at Jo. 'Though she'd kept a secret or two about herself. She's the daughter of the man behind Logan Development, but didn't want the poor gardener to know her daddy had pots of money.'

'You know why,' she said hotly. 'I wanted to be liked for myself.'

'And March wanted to be liked as plain Mr Clement. How romantic!' said Hetty, entranced, then sighed. 'Before I drink more tea I just have to take a look at Rufus.'

March nodded. 'He's in my room. But try not to disturb him, Hetty.'

'*Moi*? Of course not. I shall be as quiet as a mouse.'

'In those boots?'

Hetty promptly heaved them off, and padded away in socks the bright orange of her sweater. 'Back in a tick.'

March smiled as the door closed behind her. 'So you've met all my family now, Joanna Logan. I think it's time you introduced me to yours.'

'You're rushing me again!'

'I see no point in wasting time. I'm going to marry you, Joanna Logan, so get used to the idea.'

Jo eyed him in appeal. 'March, I need time for that. Give me a month of getting to know each other better.'

'I shan't change my mind. Ever.' March got up and stalked round the table to take her face in his hands. 'I care for you deeply, Joanna. I promise to make you a good husband. But at the end of this month you insist on either you wear my ring or I'm gone. For good.'

Jo's heart turned over at the note of finality she'd heard once before, and for a moment she was tempted to say yes to whatever he wanted. But something stubbornly independent in her make-up refused to let her. 'Understood.'

'Good.' He went back to his place as Hetty returned, looking anxious.

'He looks terrible, March. Cal's not joining me for a day or two, so I think I'd better take Rufus to Sonning with me tomorrow and feed him up.'

'Good idea—if he'll go. He's pretty hostile towards me at present.'

'Why?'

'Dog-in-the-manger attitude. The news that Jo belongs to me didn't go down well.'

Jo eyed him militantly. 'Just for the record, I don't *belong* to anyone.'

March looked down his nose at her. 'Oh, yes, you do. As I keep saying, you just need to get used to the idea.'

Hetty chuckled. 'I suppose March has told you I'm always lining up some female for him? Any one of them would jump at the chance to be Lady Arnborough. But he—in typical March fashion, of course—manages to find the one solitary woman who isn't keen on the idea.'

Jo shook her head. 'Let me put you straight on that. I *am* keen on March. Very much so.'

Hetty beamed. 'Well, then, just bite the bullet and take him with all his faults. Compared with most men, he doesn't have many.'

'Thank you, sister dear,' said March dryly.

'It's true. Normally I wouldn't say that to your face, of course, but your lady here needs to keep things in perspective. She would be marrying *you*, March, not the title.' Hetty suddenly reached across to pat Jo's hand. 'Sorry. Here I am interfering, and I'm not even your sister-in-law. Yet.'

Jo laughed. 'Don't apologise. You give good advice.'

'I am, as always, delighted to see you, Hetty,' said March dryly, 'but why are you here? I thought you were coming next week.'

Hetty sighed. 'I'm chairperson of the Arnborough branch of a cancer research charity. The place we booked for the annual ball had a fire last week, would you believe? Easthope Court can't oblige on the date, and neither can any other place with a ballroom. Because the orchestra and caterers are already booked, Candia Birkett, my co-organiser, is tearing her hair.' Hetty smiled limpidly at her brother. 'Please say we can have it here, March.'

'Why didn't she come direct to me?' he demanded.

'Because you make her nervous,' retorted his sister, and grinned at Jo. 'Candia is one of the wannabe Lady Arnboroughs.'

'Of course you expect the venue for free,' groaned March.

'It's a good cause, darling.'

'When do you want it?'

'Saturday week.' Hetty fixed him with supplicating gold eyes. 'Please say you haven't booked something else here on that date!'

'Luckily, no,' he said grimly, and sighed. 'All right. As long as you come back here next week to organise it. The last thing I want is Candia Birkett under my feet.'

Hetty flew into his arms, hugging him tightly. 'Thank you, March. You're a hero. I'll take Rufus off to Sonning for a few days first, then come back and arrange everything. Cal will be joining me next week, so you won't be a lone defenceless male.'

March turned to Jo with a grin. 'And I can keep my promise to waltz with you.'

'Something you may live to regret,' she said, pulling a face.

'Hetty, I'm sorry to rush away, but I was supposed to have

lunch with my family today. I'd like to spend a few minutes with them on my way home,' said Jo, a few hours later.

The gold eyes widened. 'You stayed here to help March instead? Thank you, Joanna.'

'I was glad to provide some moral support. But if I leave now I can read my little sister Kitty her bedtime story, and indulge in baby worship before I go to my place.'

But it was a long time before Jo actually got away. Hetty demanded every detail of the new baby, and the entire family. 'I would so like to meet them,' she said, as she kissed Jo goodbye. 'I shall send them invitations to the ball. And now,' she added, intercepting a look from her brother, 'I shall pop up to check on Rufus while you two say your goodbyes.'

When she'd gone March took Jo in his arms. 'Must you desert me so soon?'

'With Hetty for company you're not in the least deserted,' she said, unmoved. 'Will Rufus go with her to Sonning, do you think?'

'If Hetty has her way he will. He obviously needs looking after, and she's always been the best one to handle him.' March's grasp tightened. 'But let's forget my family for a moment. I'll come to your place tomorrow evening to report. And don't even think of cooking. We can order in.'

'But if Hetty's still here—'

'She can care for Rufus—and if she's taken him with her there's no problem anyway.' He silenced her with a hard, demanding kiss. 'I need time with you. Alone. And not just to go to bed. Though if that's on offer…'

Jo eyed him through her lashes. 'It might be.'

Her words won her such a lengthy kiss it took a lot of tactful coughing from Hetty to break them apart.

Jo drove to her parents' home in thoughtful mood, and arrived at Mill House just as Kitty was finishing her supper. After lots of hugging and kissing, Jo gave in to imperious demands to help with bathtime and read a story afterwards.

'Right. Let's have a proper explanation,' said Jack, when the children were in bed. 'Why did you have to stay with His Lordship today? Aren't we common folk good enough for you any more?'

'Jack!' remonstrated Kate. 'Can't you see the girl's tired? If she wants to tell us, fine, but if not leave her in peace.'

But, aware that Jack's manner hid genuine anxiety, Jo gave them the full version of the events of the day. At the first mention of Charlie Peel both parents bristled.

'If he gives you the slightest trouble again,' said Jack grimly, 'refer him to me. I'll make damn sure he never bothers you again.'

'I think March reserves that pleasure for himself, Dad. He was ready to beat him up today when he heard about my struggle with Charlie the night of the accident, but I managed to talk him out of it. Charlie's different these days, anyway. Older, and much more subdued. But he's involved himself with Rufus again in some way, and big brother isn't happy about it. March is coming to see me tomorrow evening, and maybe he'll learn more about it now Hetty's there. Apparently she deals best with Rufus.'

'What's she like?' asked Kate curiously. 'Is she very tweedy and aristocratic?'

Jo laughed. 'Anything but.' She explained about her rush home to rescue the arrangements for the charity ball. 'Hetty's friendly and outgoing, and obviously very fond of March.'

'You must be, too,' said Jack, 'if you stayed to help him in preference to seeing your family.'

'That, Jack Logan,' said Kate sharply, 'is totally uncalled for. Even though Jo couldn't make it to cook lunch for us she still sorted it so Hazel could have her day off. You weren't put out in any way at all.'

There was an uncomfortable pause.

'I apologise, Joanna,' Jack said formally at last.

'Accepted,' she returned in kind, and got up. 'I need sleep. I'd better arrive at work on time in the morning—or my boss will accuse me of neglecting my job as well as my family.'

'You deserved that, Jack,' said Kate.

He smoothed a hand over Jo's hair. 'Sorry. I just hate to see you look so exhausted. Don't come in tomorrow if you're not up to it.' He stared in horror as tears welled in her eyes, and hugged her close. 'Darling, don't *cry*.'

'Sorry. Where's Grandpa?' said Jo, blowing her nose.

'At the golf club,' said Kate. 'Now, go straight to bed when you get home, and have a good rest. You've obviously had a tiring day.'

'Eventful, certainly,' agreed Jo, and kissed everyone goodnight.

Jo's Monday was brightened by a text from March to say he'd be with her by eight. When she arrived home, early for once, she went straight upstairs for a shower. After an interval spent on her hair and face she dressed for comfort in jeans and a baggy pink sweater, then made herself a cup of coffee while she opened her post. She glanced at her watch in surprise when the doorbell rang. March was early.

Jo threw open the door with a radiant, welcoming smile which congealed on her face when she found her visitor was Charlie Peel, sporting dark glasses and a huge scarf, and carrying a laptop. 'What on earth are *you* doing here?' she said stonily.

'Can I come in?' he said hoarsely.

'I suppose so. But you can't stay long. I'm expecting company for dinner.'

Charlie followed her into the parlour. 'This is pretty,' he commented.

Jo brushed that aside. 'Cut to the chase, Charlie. What do you want?'

'It's more a case of what I need. Namely, money.'

She laughed shortly. 'Then you've come to the wrong shop.'

'I'm not asking *you* for it, Jo. Hear me out, please. To make things up to Red I want to create a website to sell his paintings. I've visited him regularly ever since he went to Italy,' he added, 'but it's time someone else saw his work. He has enormous talent.'

Jo stared at him, utterly astounded by the news that Charlie had been in constant touch with Rufus. 'Even if the paintings actually sell,' she said at last, 'can you really see Rufus parcelling them up and sending them off to buyers?'

Charlie shook his head. 'I'm not stupid, Jo. I know he wouldn't. I would take care of that side of things for him. The poor love lives in some other world half the time.'

'And whose fault is that?' snapped Jo. 'A serious head injury can't have helped him much, can it?'

His mouth twisted. 'Don't you think I know that? But Red has forgiven me. Can't you do the same?'

'It's not easy. I was in a terrible state over Rufus's accident because I didn't stop you driving that night. But of course you didn't care a toss about that—even less that you ruined Oxford for me.'

'You're so wrong about that,' he said sombrely. 'I was shattered when you gave the course up. To be honest, I couldn't believe it. You were such a determined girl—always working all the time.'

'A girl—I quote—who didn't even know how to please a man in bed.'

Charlie's mouth twisted. 'If I said that I apologise. It was my fault, not yours.'

'Because I was a girl, not a boy?'

He swallowed. 'What do you mean?'

Jo raised an eyebrow. 'What do you think I mean?'

'You know, then.' He sat in silence for a while, defeat in every line of his body. 'I've tried to convince myself that no one does.' His head came up. 'It may be an enlightened world for some these days, but not for my parents. Have you always known?'

'Of course not,' she said scathingly. 'I thought you were my boyfriend, Charlie. In the beginning I could hardly believe my luck about that. So when the bed part was disappointing I took it for granted that I wasn't sexy enough. It's taken a long time for someone to convince me otherwise.' She sat down. 'Take the sofa, Charlie, and tell me why you're here.'

He sighed. 'I had enough money—more than enough—to set up a top quality website myself. But it…went.'

Jo frowned. 'Went where?'

He removed the scarf and sunglasses to reveal two black eyes, and his painful smile revealed gaps where a couple of teeth were missing.

She gasped in horror. '*Charlie!* What on earth happened to you?'

'I had the bright idea of adding to the money by playing poker. I got into debt.' Charlie shuddered. 'After I got home today a couple of heavies came to my flat, demanding payment in full. They escorted me to my bank, where they waited while I drew out every cent I had. Then they took me back to the flat and did me over pretty thoroughly. Just so I knew they meant what they said.'

'Good God, Charlie!' Jo examined him more closely. 'Are you badly hurt? Is anything broken other than the teeth?'

'One of my ribs is cracked, but I'll live. I'll have to tell Dad I was mugged. The worst part was ringing Red to let him know I couldn't put up the money after all.' Charlie eyed her in appeal. 'From what I saw yesterday, March is pretty keen on you, Jo. Couldn't you persuade him I've turned over a new leaf? I really want to help his brother sell his paintings. I honestly believe it would do Red a whole lot of good health-wise.' He smiled ruefully. 'He's pretty surprised about you and March, by the way. He had a crush on you in the old days.'

'Whereas you desperately wanted him to have a crush on *you*, Charlie?'

He nodded miserably. 'Don't worry. I know there's not a hope in hell of that. But I'll settle for his friendship, Jo. I want to make it up to Red for the accident. And helping him to be a commercially successful artist is about the only way I know how.' He opened the laptop and booted it up. 'Take a look, Jo. I photographed some of his work.'

Jo watched, fascinated, as he scrolled through a series of sun-drenched Italian landscapes depicted with an artistry that took her breath away. 'Wow, Charlie, these are incredible! Has March seen them?'

'I tried to show him yesterday evening, after I'd spent some time with Red, but Lord Arnborough brushed me off and showed me out through his fourteenth-century door,' said Charlie bitterly, and closed the laptop.

'How much do you need?'

'A couple of thousand at the very least,' he muttered, his eyes falling. 'I had twice that, but like a fool I gambled to make it more, and lost.'

Jo whistled. 'Can't your father oblige?'

He started cracking his knuckles again. 'I'd rather raise it some other way. The family business isn't doing so well right now. Besides, I've given him more than enough grief in the past.'

Jo picked up her handbag and took out her chequebook. 'Look, I'll take a leap of faith and lend you the money myself—if only to help Rufus. I'll give you my e-mail address and you can send me the pictures so I can show March.'

Charlie looked at the cheque, blinking tears from his puffy eyes. 'I'll pay you back, I promise. I'll never forget this.'

'Neither will I,' she said tartly. 'I'll probably regret it the minute you're gone.'

Charlie thrust the cheque in his pocket, mopped his face, then collected his glasses and scarf and made for the door. He paused. 'Just to set the record straight, I did love you, Jo, in my own way. Still do.' He met her eyes for a moment. 'At least now you know why I drank so much. I've been in denial all my life. I'd say to hell with it and come out, but Red's straight. I can't take the risk of losing him.' He sighed miserably. 'I've loved him from our first day at school.'

'Oh, Charlie!' she said sadly, and gave him a hug.

He drew in a shaky breath, then buried his face on her shoulder, his body racked with sobs. She drew him down on the sofa and held him close until he was calmer, but it was a long time before he raised his head to show swollen eyes full of remorse.

'Sorry to blub like a kid,' he apologised thickly. 'It's been a bloody awful day.'

Jo kissed his bruised cheek, then pulled him to his feet. 'Time to go, Charlie. And for God's sake drive carefully.'

'Don't worry,' he said ruefully. 'My boy-racer days ended with the accident. Goodbye, Jo, and thanks again.'

She followed him into the hall and closed her front door behind him, hoping she hadn't made a huge mistake. Where Charlie was concerned, it wouldn't be the first time. But there was something about him turning over a new leaf which rang true.

As she drew the curtains in the parlour she saw a familiar tall shape pass the window and ran to open the front door, smiling radiantly.

'Hello, Joanna,' said March, in a tone which switched her smile off. 'I saw Charles Peel driving away as I arrived.'

'Yes, you did,' she said, deflated, and went ahead of him into the parlour.

'What did he want?'

'Money.'

'From you?'

'Not exactly. He wanted me to persuade you to give him money for a website for Rufus.'

'A creative way of asking for cash,' said March coldly. 'Go on, then. Start persuading me.'

'I told him he had no hope after what had happened to Rufus. Do sit down,' she added politely.

March stayed on his feet. 'Did he honestly think I'd put up money for some website?'

'If it was to sell Rufus's paintings, he hoped you might.'

'What fool would give him money for something like that?'

'A fool like me. He showed me the paintings on his laptop, and they're so wonderful I lent Charlie the money.'

March's smile turned her blood cold. 'No wonder he was so appreciative. Close your curtains in future. I was across the road parking the car, with a bird's eye view of a very touching little scene.'

'It wasn't a *love* scene, March—as you know perfectly well,' she said scornfully, and explained about the gambling debt and Charlie's injuries. 'He's a mess. When I gave him the cheque he broke down, so I comforted him a bit.'

His eyes narrowed. 'I thought you hated him.'

She sighed. 'I did. But now I truly believe Charlie is desperate to make reparation. And helping Rufus to get recognition for his talent is his way of going about it. He was always a whiz with computers, and he's experienced in marketing through his work with the family firm, so maybe he'll be successful.' Jo shot a look at the dark, shuttered face. 'You're obviously angry with me.'

He arched a sardonic eyebrow. 'After seeing your former lover in your arms, can you blame me?'

'No,' she snapped. 'I don't blame you. I blame myself for not drawing the curtains.' Her chin lifted. 'How *is* Rufus?'

'Better than yesterday—which is not saying much. But right now he's probably tucked up in bed in one of Hetty's guestrooms. She took him off—protesting—to Sonning this afternoon.' March's eyes softened. 'You look tired, Joanna.'

'Mondays tend to be tiring. For obvious reasons this one was more tiring than usual.'

'Did you call in to see your parents last night?'

She nodded. 'Jack was not hugely pleased with me for staying at Arnborough yesterday instead of going to Mill House.'

'How about your mother?'

'Kate understood that I had to help.'

'So is your father still angry with you?'

'No. For once I burst into tears—which cut him to pieces.' Jo smiled sardonically. 'Perhaps I should try the same tactics with you.'

March's mouth twisted. 'I'm sorry, Joanna.'

'No need to be. Jack and I are fine now.'

'I meant I'm sorry for my jealousy of young Peel.'

She shook her head impatiently. 'You know he's not interested in me that way.'

'Maybe not now, but he was your lover once.'

'Even then I was only a substitute for the lover he really wanted.'

March got up and pulled her to her feet. 'You're the one *I* want.' He eyed her warily. 'So are *we* fine again, too?'

Jo looked up at him thoughtfully. 'I don't know. Do you suffer much from an Othello complex?'

He released her abruptly. 'No,' he said shortly.

'You mean Lavinia never gave you cause?'

'Leave Lavinia out of it,' he said irritably. 'I'm concerned with you and Peel.'

'For heaven's sake, March, you were the one who told me Charlie was gay!'

'In which case why the hell doesn't the fool come out in the open? That way he'd have some hope of a real relationship!'

'Charlie won't come out because he's afraid to lose Rufus.'

'I doubt that he'd care.' March smiled sardonically. 'Rufus would probably say *So what?* and carry on painting.'

'Charlie will never risk that.' Joanna yawned suddenly. 'Sorry. As I said, it's been a tiring day.'

'Does that mean you want me to go?'

'No. But go, by all means, if you prefer.'

For answer, March yanked her into his arms and kissed her until her head reeled. 'Of course I don't want to go,' he growled. 'Right now I want to carry you to your bed and make love to you until we forget my brother and Charlie and everything else in the world other than you and me, Joanna Logan.'

To her horror her stomach gave such an unromantic rumble March laughed. 'But first I'd better feed you. What would you like?'

Jo's eyes danced. 'I really fancy some fish and chips.'

As they ate their meal at the kitchen table later Jo teased him unmercifully. 'I wish I'd gone with you—just to see Lord Arnborough standing in line for fish and chips!'

March was unmoved. 'It wasn't the first time. Though luxuries like fish and chips were pretty rare in my life when I was a student. I tried to manage without asking my father for hand-outs, so bowls of cereal and baked beans straight from the can were more my thing.'

'You're kidding!'

'Certainly not. Cheap, filling and nourishing—and sometimes I even had the beans on toast. How about you?'

'In my Oxford days I ate in the refectory. Toasters were banned in the rooms, and there was no kitchen in my hall.'

'Life must have been a lot different when you transferred to college here. Peel's fault,' he added.

Jo shook her head. 'Something Charlie said tonight has rather changed my mind about that. He was utterly sure I was the determined type who would finish no matter what. Much as it grieves me to agree with him, he's right.' Jo sighed as she collected plates. 'I should have stuck it out and graduated.'

'Do you regret that now?'

'Only because I didn't finish what I started. My business

qualifications are far more practical career-wise. And what I'm doing now with Jack suits me down to the ground.'

March got to his feet, his eyes sombre as they followed her. 'Which is going to work against me, of course.'

Jo stacked the plates in the dishwasher then turned to face him. 'In what way?'

'I want you with me at Arnborough. You can hardly commute from there to keep working for your father, Joanna.'

'I know. Which is precisely why I've asked you for time.' She yawned again. 'Sorry. I've had a busy day—and evening.'

'Me too,' said March, and kissed her. 'Let's go to bed.'

'I thought you just wanted to talk!'

'I want to hold you in my arms while we do.'

When Jo showed him into her room March grinned. 'What a bed!'

'Kate's maiden aunt left it to her. Though I think *single* is the word rather than maiden.' Jo smoothed a loving hand over the curved footboard. 'I can't believe she always slept alone in it, like me.'

'Not like you tonight, my darling,' he said huskily, and picked her up to lay her on the bed.

With senses heightened by their quarrel, their loving was feverishly short—but so utterly fulfilling they lay entwined together afterwards, savouring the pure pleasure of being together as March whispered some very satisfying things in Jo's ear.

'Time for the talk,' he said at last, and raised her hand to his lips. 'You know that I can't offer you a very luxurious lifestyle. My assets are all I have.'

'That part of it wouldn't worry me at all—if we do marry.'

'Of course we're going to marry. You're mine, Joanna Logan,' said March, and began to make love to her in a way designed to remove any last lingering doubts she might have on the subject.

* * *

Jo rang Isobel next day, and arranged to spend the evening at her flat over a bottle of wine and whatever fast food she desired.

'I need your opinion,' said Jo that night, when only pizza crusts were left.

Isobel's blonde curls and cornflower-blue eyes often misled the uninformed about the brain behind them. At that moment the blue gaze was trained like a laser on her friend. 'About your love-life?'

'No. I'll sort that for myself.'

'Thank goodness for that. So, what's up?'

Jo reached for the laptop she'd brought with her. 'Some pictures were e-mailed to me today.'

'Not naughty ones, I hope!'

'Certainly not. These are paintings. And in my opinion they're good.'

'Then they probably are. Let me see.'

Jo opened up the laptop and brought Rufus Clement's paintings up on the screen.

Isobel looked at each one in complete concentration as Jo put the laptop in slide-show mode. 'Who painted these?' she asked, going through them for the second time.

'Rufus Clement—March's brother. What do you think?'

Isobel blew out her cheeks. 'I can't say for sure, without seeing them in the flesh, as it were, but they're good. Really, really good. So what's this tale of woe you hinted at on the phone?'

Jo launched into the saga of Charlie and the website.

Isobel heard her out, then nodded. 'He could sell the paintings that way, of course. But if Charlie's going to act for Rufus Clement as his business manager why doesn't he arrange an exhibition first?'

'You mean in this country?'

'It would be a bit coals-to-Newcastle to arrange one in Florence. Plenty of paintings there already, darling.'

Jo laughed. 'So where, then?'

'In my gallery downstairs, for starters. Plenty of interest—reasonably local artist and so on—and his aristocratic connections wouldn't hurt, either. Or,' Isobel added with a dramatic pause, 'they could be shown at the family seat. There must be a likely venue in your lover's stately home.'

'How do you know he's my lover?'

The blue eyes looked sceptical. 'Are you going to tell me this March of yours is just a friend?'

'No.' Jo gave her friend a wry smile. 'In fact, he wants to marry me.'

Isobel's answering screech was deafening. 'You're going to be Lady whatever-it-is?'

'It's Lady Arnborough—which I'd rather not be.'

'You haven't gone all socialist all of a sudden, have you?' demanded Isobel. 'Why shouldn't you be Lady Arnborough?'

Jo thrust a hand through her hair. 'It's not just the title, Bel, it's everything that goes with it.'

'March goes with it, which is the most important thing. Are you in love with him?'

'Yes.'

'Is he in love with you?'

'That's the rub,' admitted Jo with a sigh. 'He assures me I'm ideal for the post of wife—because I'm intelligent and capable and so on. To blazes with capable! I want him to be crazily in love with me, Bel. Am I asking too much?'

'Are you good together in bed?'

Jo flushed. 'Yes.'

Isobel beamed. 'Then for heaven's sake grab him and live happily ever after. When do I get to meet him?'

'How would you like to go to a ball, Cinderella?'

CHAPTER TWELVE

DUE to its surprise relocation to Arnborough Hall, the charity ball promised to be the event of the season. But when the invitation arrived at Mill House Jo couldn't persuade her mother to accept.

'It's too soon after Tom's arrival, darling,' Kate said firmly. 'Both for my figure and my energy. But there's no reason why Jack can't go.'

'He won't without you!'

Jo was right. Jack Logan gave his daughter a very extravagant cheque—enough to cover the cost of a ball dress and a donation to the charity—but much preferred to stay home with his wife. 'You'll have Isobel for company on the journey, Jo,' he told her, and grinned. 'And you'll enjoy yourself far more without your father keeping tabs on you.'

To her dismay, Jo saw nothing of March for the week before the ball because, to his intense irritation, he'd caught—as he complained to her thickly—a very unromantic cold.

'So to be up to par for the big event I'm dosing myself with pills and keeping out of everyone's way. Which is driving me mad while Hetty and her crew cause mayhem everywhere.'

'Look on the bright side. You're avoiding Candia Birkett.'

He gave a snort of laughter which turned into a hacking cough. 'Sorry!' he said breathlessly. 'I can't remember when I last had a cold. I'm feeling sorry for myself, Joanna.'

'I can tell.'

'I miss you like hell.'

'I miss you too. So hurry up and get better. I've splashed out on a very expensive dress, and I'd hate to waste it.'

'You wouldn't come if I'm not fit to turn up?'

'Of course I wouldn't,' she said scornfully.

'I feel better already. Come early on Saturday—before all the others.'

'Will do. How's Rufus?'

'Keeping out of the way at Sonning. Though Hetty's insisting he turns up on Saturday.'

'Good. He can talk shop with Isobel.'

'I can think of better things to do with you,' said March huskily.

'You're supposed to be ill!'

'A cold, it seems, does not damp down the libido,' he informed her. 'I want you *bad*, Joanna. Be warned—I'm hellish tired of this waiting game.'

His parting shot was hard to forget—even when Isobel joined her in Park Crescent to get ready for the ball together.

'We look pretty damned good,' said Isobel, as they finally stood together in front of a cheval mirror.

'We certainly do,' agreed Jo. 'On my first visit to Arnborough I fancied myself twirling round the ballroom there in a dress something like this. Never thought it would happen.'

'But it has. And a lot more could happen if you'd stop dragging your heels about marrying March,' said Isobel bluntly. 'He won't be able to take his eyes off you in that creation.'

Jo eyed herself doubtfully. 'I'm not sure now that I should have gone for strapless. You don't think the cut is too low?'

'Only in your dad's eyes. Your mother thinks it's perfect. Your man will, too.' Isobel eyed her own asymmetric layers of chiffon critically. 'Why do I always end up buying blue?'

'Because it looks good with your eyes!' Jo smiled a little as she held out her flowing topaz satin skirt to curtsey to her reflection. 'Whereas mine is the exact shade of my Lord Arnborough's.'

'Oh, I see!' Isobel laughed and gave her a hug. 'That's why you shelled out a small fortune for it.'

'Right, then,' said Jo, suddenly on fire with excitement as the limousine came to collect them. 'Time we were off to the ball.'

The weather had answered Hetty's prayers, and a full moon was painting a wide silver path over the waters of the moat as they were driven through the floodlit grounds at Arnborough.

'My God,' breathed Isobel as they left the car. 'What a magical place, Jo.'

'Yes,' said Jo tersely, her stomach cramping with sudden nerves.

Then the doors were thrown open and March, tall, dark and unbelievably handsome in formal black and white, came hurrying to take Jo in his arms and press a lingering kiss on both cheeks. Then he gave her a look which made it clear he wanted to kiss a lot more of her than that. 'You look very, very beautiful, Miss Logan,' he said huskily, and released her to smile at Isobel. 'So do you, Miss James. Welcome to Arnborough.'

'Thank you for inviting me to this wonderful home of yours,' Isobel told him, standing back to survey it with an artist's eye.

'Are you feeling better, March?' asked Jo.

'I am now you're here,' he assured her as they entered the warmth and welcome of the Great hall, which was already packed with people as waiters circulated through the crowd of convivial guests laughing and talking at full volume—which stopped dramatically as March appeared with a girl on each arm.

Hetty, in clinging strapless black worn with a diamond pendant, rushed forward to hug Joanna, and turned with her irresistible smile to welcome Isobel. 'Hi, I'm March's sister, Hetty. Let me introduce you to everyone. First and most importantly to my husband, Calvin Stern. Cal—meet Miss Joanna Logan and Miss Isobel James.'

Cal Stern, long of leg and kind of face, his eyes twinkling behind gold-rimmed glasses, greeted them both with friendly warmth before Hetty swept Jo and Isobel off to meet Candia Birkett and the rest of the charity committee, plus their assorted husbands and partners.

March rescued them a few minutes later. 'Forgive me for stealing them, everyone, but my guests must be thirsty.' He found them drinks, then led them over to introduce Isobel to Rufus, in front of the great fireplace, and smoothly isolated them into a private group of six with Hetty and Cal.

'You're the artist,' Isobel said to Rufus, and raised her glass in salute. 'I'm deeply impressed by your work.'

'Isobel owns an art gallery. She's also a very accomplished watercolourist,' said Jo, as Rufus flushed in response to the compliment, looking a lot more like the boy she remembered.

'You really think I'm any good?' he asked Isobel.

'Why don't you two talk painting for a while?' said March. 'I want to show Joanna the ballroom. Hetty, I'll leave you and Cal to deal with the people in here. There's half an hour to go before the actual dancing.'

'You go on, love,' said his sister, patting his hand. She smiled at Jo. 'He's been feeling pretty rough, Joanna. He needs some tender loving care.'

Conscious that all eyes were on them as March took her from the Great Hall into the vestibule, Jo fluttered her eyelashes at him when he hurried her up the staircase instead of to the ballroom. 'Are you carrying me off to your tower, Lord Arnborough?'

'Can't wait to get that far,' he muttered, and rushed her up the private branch of stairs and along the landing to his bedroom. He shut the door. 'Do you have a lipstick in that excuse for a handbag?'

'Yes.'

'Thank God,' he said, and pulled her into his arms to kiss

and caress her with hunger fuelled by their ten-day separation, his eyes glittering into hers as he raised his head at last. 'I missed you, Joanna.'

'I missed you too,' she said breathlessly, and smiled shakily. 'But now I need a minute or two for repairs, and then you'd better show me the ballroom. Hetty's bound to ask what I think of it.'

March kissed her fleetingly again, the raw tension fading from his face as he stood back to look at her in slow scrutiny from head to toe. 'Glorious dress.'

'I'm glad you like it.' Jo twitched the top back up into place over breasts throbbing from his caresses. 'Now, let me have a minute in front of your mirror, and then we must go back. Isobel will think I've deserted her.'

'She's almost as beautiful as you,' commented March, watching as Jo repaired her lipstick. 'And if she can talk art with him Rufus will stick to her like glue. I try to take an interest, but sometimes his tunnel vision about the subject is a bit hard to take. Hetty has more patience than me.'

'I like her husband—he reminds me of someone,' said Jo, and scrubbed lipstick from his mouth with a tissue, her breath catching as he sucked on her finger.

'I always think Cal's a bit like Gary Cooper in glasses,' said March, as they started back downstairs. 'Or are you too young to remember him?'

'Of course not. Who can forget *High Noon*?' she retorted, then smiled in delight as they reached the dining room, which looked very different from its daytime persona. It was festive, with flowers everywhere, and caterers hurrying about in preparation for the buffet supper that would be served during the interval. 'This room looks so much less daunting now it's in party mood.'

'I've never thought of it as daunting,' he said, surprised.

'Because you've lived with it all your life.' She smiled at him. 'Come on. I want to see the ballroom in party mood, too.'

The ladies of the Arnborough branch of the charity had done long-dead Aurelia proud. The ballroom was a scene straight out of Cinderella, with great displays of flowers foaming out of urns along the walls and either side of the dais, where the band was in the process of setting up. Small tables surrounded by gilt chairs were arranged in groups around the walls, and overhead the newly cleaned chandeliers gleamed like waterfalls of diamonds, their light reflected in the gleaming floor and in the long windows which formed the two outer walls of the ballroom.

'How absolutely magnificent,' said a hushed voice behind them, and Jo turned to smile at Isobel, who was standing with Rufus, her eyes wide as she drank in the scene. 'But it looks so familiar, Jo.'

'Probably spotted it in a film,' said Rufus prosaically. 'March is always hiring the place out to some film company or other.'

'Great location to exhibit your pictures,' said Isobel. 'Don't you agree, March?'

'I do,' he assured her. 'Any time Rufus wants. But right now its function is to bring Hetty and her coven money for their charity. Let's rejoin them for a minute or two. I must do my meeting and greeting bit for a while with Hetty. I suppose it's no use asking you to join in, Rufus.'

His brother blanched at the thought. 'I thought I'd take Isobel up to the long gallery and show her our art collection.'

'As long as you bring her back sooner rather than later,' said Jo, and grinned. 'And then you have to dance with her. And with me.'

Rufus looked less appalled by the prospect than expected. 'Only too happy. But don't expect me to dance with Candia Birkett.'

'Poor woman—why not?' said Isobel. 'She seemed rather charming.'

'She was at school with Hetty, and at one time she was

forever wangling invitations to Arnborough.' Rufus leered at his brother. 'She had designs on March.'

'Quiet,' growled March as they reached the Great Hall. 'Candia fancies herself as a collector these days, and she's not short of cash. She might buy one of your paintings.'

Rescued from a session of social intermingling, Jo and Isobel managed to eat a couple of much-needed canapés from a tray Cal appropriated from a waiter.

'It's a long time until supper,' he reminded them.

'True,' said March, helping himself to a couple of morsels. He smiled at Jo. 'You need to bolster up your strength for that first waltz with me.'

'I don't waltz very well,' she warned.

'Don't worry, honey, neither do I,' said Cal. 'But when Hetty says dance, I dance. The Clement family is big on giving orders.'

'I've noticed,' agreed Jo, sending a sparkling look at March.

'Perhaps,' said Isobel, smiling at him, 'you'd do better with a request than an order?'

He grinned. 'I'll have to try it some time.'

'The band has begun to play,' said Hetty. 'Brace yourselves, everyone—it's showtime.'

Rufus promptly sneaked Isobel out of the main door. 'I'll take her up by way of the tower stairs.'

'I just hope she'll be fit to dance afterwards,' said Jo, as she went into the vestibule with March. 'I'll keep in the background.'

He raised a sardonic eyebrow. 'Coward. Hide behind us with Cal, then. He doesn't like the meeting and greeting bit, either.'

For a while it was one long repetition of greeting and handshaking while Jo talked to Cal, grateful for his company.

'We should have escaped up to the gallery with Isobel and Rufus,' he said in an undertone.

'I wasn't brave enough to suggest it,' she said candidly.

'Neither was I, babe!'

Jo stiffened as she saw a familiar pair come into the vestibule. Mr and Mrs Jeremy Fox-Hatton were the last to arrive, and made the grand entrance Lavinia had obviously intended. She swept in, bestowing smiles all round, and flung her coat to a steward, revealing beaded crimson silk that clung like a second skin.

Just like a snake, thought Jo uncharitably.

'Darling,' said Lavinia, in a voice intended to carry, 'how lovely to see you again.' She cast herself into March's reluctant arms, gave him a smacking kiss on both cheeks, then turned to Hetty, who very pointedly kissed the air a foot away from Lavinia's cheek and evaded her embrace.

'Hello, Lavinia.' Hetty smiled past her. 'Jerry, how lovely to see *you*.'

'Ouch,' said Cal quietly.

To Jo's horror, March reached out a hand and drew her close. 'Allow me to present Miss Joanna Logan.'

Lavinia's eyes narrowed as she took in Jo's dress. 'We've already met, March.'

'Have you? I'd forgotten.' He turned to Cal. 'And this is my brother-in-law—Calvin Stern.'

'I've met Mr Stern too,' said Lavinia acidly, as Cal gave a surprisingly graceful bow.

'Frightfully sorry,' said March, coolly insincere. 'My memory must be going. Do go on in.'

'Wow,' said Hetty, grinning at her husband.

'Wow's the word,' he agreed. 'Your brother sure knows how to freeze people off.'

'It's a gift,' she agreed, and smiled at Cal with relish. 'I can do it too, when I try.'

'Don't try it with me, sweetheart,' he threatened, and received a smile which rocked him on his heels.

'Never with you, my darling.'

'Come on, you two,' ordered March. 'I have a speech to make before the ball can officially start rolling.'

'We'll take care of you,' Hetty assured Jo as they went into the ballroom, which looked no less magical now it was full of people.

'I hope Rufus will bring Isobel back soon,' said Jo, as March leapt up on the stage.

'They're probably arguing the rival merits of Lawrence and Gainsborough, or whoever,' said Hetty with a grin. 'Don't worry. Your friend is safe with Rufus.'

March smiled on the assembled crowd, waited for silence, then welcomed everyone to the annual fundraiser for the local branch of the charity, and stepped down from the stage to make for Joanna as couples surged onto the floor to dance.

'This is mine, I believe,' he said, smiling down at her.

Feeling like Cinderella singled out by the Prince, Jo took his hand and went into his arms for the opening waltz. 'I'll have to count to keep in time,' she said in his ear, 'I'm not very good at this kind of thing.'

But to her surprise Jo found she was better at conventional ballroom dancing with March than on any of the rare occasions she'd had a shot at it in the past.

'You lie,' he said, his breath warm against her cheek. 'You dance like a dream, Joanna.'

It felt like a dream as she revolved with him under the sparkling chandeliers, exactly as she'd imagined. Though her imagination had never come up with Lord Arnborough as her partner. But the very unreality of it all was the problem. All this was so alien to her normal life it was impossible to picture herself as part of it on a regular basis. But she might as well enjoy the dream while it lasted.

She had the next dance with Cal, and a third with Rufus, and found that she was not as good with either of them as with March. She was grateful to sit out with Hetty and Isobel when March went off to do his duty with some of the organizers—including Candia Birkett, whose plain face lit up like a Christmas tree as she danced with him.

'Poor woman. She's been in love with him for years,' said Hetty.

'Hardly surprising. Your brother's a charmer,' said Isobel, watching him.

'Do you agree with that, Jo?' said his loving sister.

'Yes.'

'You know he's determined to marry you?'

'Yes.'

'And March,' said Hetty ruthlessly, 'is used to getting what he wants.'

'Not with Lavinia,' Jo reminded her.

'Pooh! That was just sex-based infatuation, and he soon got over it.' Hetty patted her hand. 'Whereas *you* would be the ideal wife for him.'

'I know. Clever and capable,' said Jo, resigned. 'I can even cook.'

Isobel moved closer in instant sympathy. 'He sees a lot more in you than that, love.'

Hetty stared at Jo in surprise. 'Darling, March really cares for you.'

'Yes, I know.'

'Then what's the problem?'

'Nothing you can put right, Hetty,' said Jo, and pinned a smile on her face as a drum roll preceded the band leader's announcement that supper was served in the dining room.

March rejoined them, smiling. 'Come with me, ladies. Our supper's waiting us in the family dining room. I've sent Cal and Rufus on ahead.'

'Oh, how lovely,' sighed Hetty. 'I didn't fancy standing in line.'

'Thank God for food,' said Rufus, when they joined him in the small vaulted room. 'I'm not used to all this exercise.'

'You dance surprisingly well, then,' said Isobel, picking up a plate. 'Yum, this looks wonderful.'

It was restful to share the party food in private. Jo felt

relaxed for the first time all evening as she sat between March and Isobel.

'So, what did you think of the paintings in the long gallery?' she asked her friend.

'Very interesting. Some of them are merely the school of or the style of famous artists, but it was great to see a genuine Lawrence *and* a Gainsborough. Though the portrait that interested me most was the Constable.'

Jo nodded. 'I was surprised when I spotted it. Because he's known for landscapes, its rarity must make it valuable.'

'He kept to his family and friends as subjects,' said Rufus. 'Unlike the society painters, like Lawrence, in Constable's day his name on a portrait didn't carry the same cachet.'

'How did you manage on the spiral stairs, Isobel?' asked March. 'Joanna complained the first time I took her up.'

'I went up barefoot,' said Isobel, laughing.

'I guess you have a lot in common with Rufus,' said Cal, smiling at her. 'Jo tells me you like his work.'

'A lot,' she agreed. 'I wish I could paint half as well.'

'You're too modest,' said March emphatically. 'The watercolours you painted for Joanna are exquisite.'

'But after looking at Rufus's work I really want to try oil,' she said, and turned to him. 'Exactly *how* do you get that extraordinary light in your sky?'

'That's it,' said Hetty, as her younger brother launched into his favourite subject. 'We'll never get him back to the ballroom now.'

Rufus turned in sharp dismay. 'There's more dancing?'

'Oh, yes,' said March relentlessly. 'Hetty's brought in a rock band for modern stuff after the supper break, and you can hop around with everyone else. *Noblesse oblige* and all that.'

At the end of the evening Jo was so tired by the time the band played the last dance she began to droop in March's arms.

'So,' he said in her ear, 'have you enjoyed twirling around under my chandeliers?'

'Oh, yes.' She smiled brightly. 'Cinderella has had a great time. But the party's over now. My fairy coach is waiting.'

He pulled her closer. 'I wish you'd agree to stay here.'

'I can't let Isobel go back alone.'

'I have another speech to make before everyone goes home. Don't go away.'

As the band came to a final crescendo March brought Jo to a stop in front of the dais, then stepped on to it and took the microphone to smile into the upturned, expectant faces.

'Ladies and gentlemen, I give you my grateful thanks for making this evening such a success for the charity. Your support, as always, is deeply appreciated. And now,' he added, 'I have an announcement of my own to make.'

To Joanna's horror, he reached down to lift her onto the stage, sending a buzz of excitement running through the room. And a look like a hot poker from the lady in red sequins.

'I'm taking this perfect opportunity to introduce Miss Joanna Logan—soon to be my wife.' He took Jo's left hand in his, slid a ring on the third finger, and then raised the hand to his lips—to a tumult of applause and loud shouts of congratulation from all sides. 'Thank you, one and all,' he shouted back, his eyes glittering with a hint of defiance behind the elation as they met Joanna's. 'Goodnight everyone, and safe journey home.'

'Excuse me, My Lord,' said one of the stewards. 'The car's arrived for Miss Logan and her friend. The driver would like to leave before the crowd.'

'Thank you.' March jumped down and lifted Joanna after him. Hetty and Cal, with Isobel and Rufus close behind, rushed to hug and kiss her and exclaim their pleasure and delight—all talking at once in such excitement that no one seemed to notice Jo's smile was fixed and she had nothing to say. March had his arm round her tightly as they left the ballroom, but none of the smiling, congratulating crowd realised he was keeping her prisoner rather than in a lover's embrace.

'I'll see you tomorrow about one, darling,' March said at last, after all the goodbyes had been said. He bent to kiss her as he helped her into the limousine, where Isobel was discreetly tucked into the far corner.

'Splendid,' said Jo, looking him in the eye. 'I'll look forward to that.'

The car had left the grounds of Arnborough and was well on the road home before Isobel reached forward to close the partition. She reached for Jo's hand and examined the cluster of diamonds on her ring finger.

'You gave in, then,' she said quietly. 'So why aren't you happy about it?'

'I didn't give in. Lord Arnborough stole a march on me—pardon the pun.' Jo's eyes flashed dangerously. 'He had no right to make the announcement like that, when I couldn't do a damn thing to stop him.'

'I think it's romantic,' said Isobel. 'He just wanted to make sure of you.'

'Then he made a big mistake,' snapped Jo. 'He knew I had doubts about marrying him. They multiplied as the evening went on. As you said, Bel, Arnborough is a magical place, but I just can't see myself as part of the fairytale.'

'Never mind your doubts about Arnborough. What are your feelings for *March*?'

'No doubts on that score. I may be in love with him every way there is, but I resent the way he took the matter out of my hands like that. I'm *not* one of his vassals!' Jo raked an unsteady hand through her hair. 'Jack won't be pleased, either. He would have expected a man like March to ask for my parents' approval first.'

'Do men still do that?'

'A man like Lord Arnborough—yes!'

* * *

It was light before Jo finally fell into a heavy sleep. She woke with a start to the sound of the doorbell. She stumbled blearily from the bed to grab her dressing gown, and went barefoot downstairs to find the last visitor she expected on her doorstep.

'Good heavens, Jo,' said Kate Logan, eyeing her daughter askance. 'You look absolutely awful. Hangover?'

'Certainly not.' Jo blinked owlishly. 'What in the world are you doing here at this hour?'

'Waiting to be asked in, for one thing. I can't stay long.'

'Sorry—sorry.' Jo yawned and closed the door. 'Put the kettle on while I go and brush my teeth. Shan't be a moment.'

When they were facing each other across the kitchen table, with two steaming mugs of coffee in front of them, Kate eyed her daughter expectantly.

'Well? Tell me all about it.'

'The ball was a great success.'

'Never mind the ball—I want to see the ring!'

Jo stiffened. 'You *know* about it?'

Kate nodded warily. 'Drink some coffee, darling. You look as though you need some caffeine.'

'Never mind the coffee—how do you know about the ring?'

'I assumed March had one ready because he rang Jack on Friday evening to ask for your hand, in the good old-fashioned way. I was burning to tell you, but he asked us not to.' Kate bit her lip. 'Are you saying he *didn't* propose to you last night after all?'

'Not exactly.' In a flat, unemotional voice Jo described his announcement from the stage.

Kate groaned. 'Bad move. His Lordship's rather shot himself in the foot, I take it?'

'Absolutely,' said Jo stonily, but her lip suddenly quivered. 'Before last night I was warming to the idea of marrying him. But the glitz and glamour of a ball at Arnborough changed my mind. I can't live that kind of life.'

'Are you in love with him?'

'Oh, yes,' said Jo miserably. 'Besotted, if you want the truth. Unfortunately my main attraction for March—apart from the bed part—is my organisational skill. Handy for helping him run Arnborough.'

'That, my darling, is a load of nonsense.' Kate got up. 'I must dash now, but we'll talk later—after lunch. To which March is invited, by the way. He's picking you up at one.'

Jo glared at her mother. 'Tell me you're not serious!'

'I asked him myself. Do you want me to ring him to cancel?'

'No. I'll do the cancelling when he comes.'

'Joanna, just be careful you don't say something you later regret,' said Kate emphatically. 'I did that once, remember? And spent thirteen long years apart from Jack as a consequence.'

Jo was trying to read the Sunday paper when March arrived. He looked tired, but dauntingly elegant in a formal suit as he held out a large bouquet of tawny roses.

'For my lady,' he said, and raised her left hand to kiss it. He tightened his grasp enough to make her wince. 'No ring?'

'Please come inside.' She put the bouquet on the hall table and led him into the parlour.

March eyed her worn jeans and faded sweatshirt quizzically. 'Am I overdressed for a celebration lunch?'

'We're not joining my parents for lunch, March, because there's nothing to celebrate.' Jo handed him the diamond ring she took from her pocket. 'So you can have this back.'

'Why?' His eyes blazed in angry disbelief. 'Is this because I jumped the gun last night?'

'It was a contributory factor,' she retorted, her own eyes angry. 'But I'd made up my mind to say no beforehand.'

He stood very still, a pulse throbbing at the corner of his mouth. 'Why? Didn't I come up to scratch as a lover?'

'Typical male response,' she said scathingly. 'Yes, March.

In fact you are such a skilled lover I'd be happy to carry on in-definitely with our present arrangement—'

'But not as my wife.'

'Exactly.'

'How flattering.' March's face hardened into a mask. 'So ul-timately you're no different from Lavinia.'

Jo coloured hotly. 'That's not true. For me, it's nothing to do with money.'

'Then what *is* the problem, Joanna?'

'I realised last night that I just couldn't do it.'

'Because I took a risk by taking the decision out of your hands?'

'I resented that—though there was no risk involved. You knew I wouldn't reject you in front of your family and friends.' She looked at him steadily. 'But before that, watching you last night at the centre of things in your own world, I couldn't see myself ever being part of it.'

'So you waited to reject me in private—for which I should be grateful, I suppose,' he cut back, and gave a mirthless laugh. 'I was so bloody tired of waiting for you to make up your mind I decided to do it for you, in what I fondly thought was as romantic a way as possible. God, what a fool!'

She licked suddenly dry lips. 'This needn't end things between us, March. We could still be—'

'If you say *good friends* I'm likely to get violent,' March said, in a tone which sent her backing away. 'Don't worry. I shan't hurt you. Nor shall I trouble you again,' he said harshly, and turned on his heel. He stopped in the doorway and turned to give her a look which sent the wrong kind of shivers down her spine. 'I very deliberately took no precautions when I made love to you, so I shall, of course, expect you to let me know if you're expecting my child.'

Jo stared at him. 'Deliberately?' she said, when she could trust her voice. 'How mortifying. And there was I thinking you were carried away by the heat of the moment.' Her chin lifted. 'Have no fear, Lord Arnborough. I shan't appear on your medieval doorstep, begging you to acknowledge your by-blow. I take responsibility for my own precautions.'

A tigerish light flared in his eyes for an instant, then snuffed out. 'I see. That would appear to be that.' He bared his teeth in a smile which chilled her to the bone. 'Please convey my regrets to your parents.'

The weeks after the ball were the most miserable of Jo's life. For once her mother had no sympathy with her, and told Jo in no uncertain terms that she had been a fool to personally sabotage her own happiness.

'You would have soon got used to life at Arnborough. And if you couldn't have made March fall hopelessly in love with you while you were at it I'd have eaten my hat,' she told Jo. 'Just because the relationship failed to tick every last one of your boxes you've thrown it away.'

Jo was only too conscious of that.

She received a distressed phone call from Hetty, demanding to know what had gone wrong, but could only explain, lamely, that she was just not cut out to be Lady Arnborough.

'Garbage,' said Henrietta Stern. 'You two were made for each other. I hate to see March so unhappy. I love him very much, you know.'

So did Jo—but it seemed unwise to mention that in the circumstances.

Isobel, desperate to give comfort, ordered the Carey twins to wangle time off on the same night for once, to give Jo some much-needed cheering up over supper at her flat. Leo and Josh did their best to oblige, plying Jo with wine and relating hair-raising medical anecdotes to make her laugh. And even though as doctors they were shocked by her weight loss, they managed to refrain from commenting on it.

Jack Logan, also helpless to find some way of comforting his daughter, suggested she take a little break somewhere—get away for a while.

'Lick my wounds on a sunny beach? No thanks, Dad. I need work, not time on my hands.'

Kate relented when she saw how much her daughter regretted sending March away, and filled her daughter's spare time with babysitting duties. She also insisted that Jo attend family meals regularly.

Slowly Jo began to recover from her self-inflicted misery. She gave herself a scathing lecture on self-pity and rejoined the living, as she put it to Isobel, who greeted the news with such relief Jo felt guilty for causing her friend so much anxiety.

This new-found tranquillity took a hammering a few weeks later. Early for her usual meeting with Isobel one Saturday, Jo was passing the time by cleaning the inside of her parlour window when a familiar sports car turned into Park Crescent. She almost fell as she scrambled down from her ladder, then waited in the hall, heart thudding and knees shaky. When the doorbell rang at last she forgot to put down her bucket as she went to the door.

Jo opened it with a polite smile that came unglued when she found that her visitor was Rufus, not March. 'Hi!' she managed. 'Isobel told me you were back from Italy. Come in.'

'Thanks. Good to see you Jo.' He eyed her bucket in amusement. 'Am I interrupting something?'

'Window-cleaning—interrupt all you like. Go into the parlour. I'll just get rid of this. Would you like a drink?'

'Nothing, thanks. I must get back soon, or milord will be worried about the light of his life out there. March must be getting soft in his old age—he's never let me drive it before.'

When Jo rejoined him, Rufus was intent on Isobel's watercolours. 'These are so good,' he said, turning. 'Isobel's wasted in her job. Why doesn't she paint full-time?'

'She likes to eat,' said Jo, wondering why he was here.

'I came to deliver some invitations,' he said, after driving Jo mad by first examining every watercolour in detail. 'Charlie's finally organised my exhibition at Arnborough, and it would mean a lot to me for you to be there, Jo. Your parents, too, if you think they'd be interested.'

'I'll ask,' said Jo, feeling almost light-headed with disappointment. Rufus was not here as March's emissary.

'But you *will* come with Isobel?' he persisted.

Oh, why not? March could hardly refuse to let her in. 'Of course I will, Rufus. I'm glad to see you looking so much better.'

'There was nothing really wrong with me,' he admitted guiltily. 'I just forget to eat when I'm painting, and the result is usually one of the headaches I've been plagued with since the accident. But now the Parisis have let Charlie share the lake house with me I'm being looked after very well. Charlie's a brilliant cook as well as an efficient manager.'

'Talents he certainly hid from me! But it's a good thing for both of you, I think.' Jo gave him a straight look. 'Look, Rufus, be kinder to Charlie than I was. He's never recovered from half-killing you that night.'

Rufus coloured painfully. 'Actually, Jo, he didn't. When he came to pick me up he was steaming over the row he'd had with you. Then he got hopping mad with me because I took your side. He was so drunk I made him give *me* the keys. I was driving when we had the accident.'

Jo stared at him in shock. 'But I thought you couldn't drive back then.'

'March had made me have driving lessons, but I hadn't passed my test. I'd had a bit to drink myself that night, too, and had a blazing row with Charlie in the car. Which is why we had the accident.' His mouth turned down. 'You probably won't believe it, but after the smack on the head I had absolutely no recall of that night. Then Charlie came to see me in Italy one day and it all came filtering back.'

'He never said a word!'

Rufus nodded ruefully. 'He was afraid it could mean a cus-todial sentence for me, so he took the blame. March was mad as hell with me when I told him. Not to mention amazed that Charlie had risked jail himself rather than tell the truth.'

'Because he loves you,' said Jo simply.

Rufus nodded, flushing slightly. 'I know. In my own way I love him too—but only as a special friend, which he says is enough. We don't sleep together, but we rub along very well now we live together. Please come to the exhibition, Jo.'

'Wouldn't miss it for the world,' she assured him.

'Nice little place,' said Jack Logan, as he drove his compan-ions into the Arnborough car park a fortnight later.

'Nice?' said Kate. 'It's magnificent! But I see what you mean, Jo. It's awe-inspiring. Exactly Kitty's idea of an enchanted castle.'

Jo was so reluctant to get out of the car Isobel gave her a push at last.

'Come on. Chin up.'

Jo was fully prepared for a cool reception from the stewards gathered outside the main doors to welcome the guests. But the woman who came to greet them was the chief steward Jo had met on her first day. She smiled kindly at Jo, gave a warm welcome to her parents and Isobel, and directed them inside, informing them that drinks were being served in the Great Hall before the viewing in the ballroom.

'Rufus didn't want anyone sloshing champagne about anywhere near his paintings,' whispered Isobel. 'I promised I'd go straight to the ballroom when we got here, so I'll sneak off now. See you later.'

To Jo's surprise Jack put an arm round her as they went inside, and she was glad of it when she noticed several faces familiar from the ball. But his protection proved unnecessary when Hetty rushed towards her, arms outstretched.

'Joanna, I'm so glad you came.'

Jo sagged a little as Hetty's arms closed her. 'I thought I'd be *persona non grata* here now,' she said thickly.

'Not with me,' Hetty assured her, and surrendered her to Cal as she smiled up at Jack. 'Hi. I'm Henrietta Stern, and the man hugging your daughter is my husband Calvin.'

Jack shook her hand, smiling. 'Delighted to meet you. Let me introduce my wife.'

Hetty stared in amazement as she shook Kate's hand. She turned to grab Cal's arm. 'Darling, can you believe that this lovely lady is actually Joanna's *mother*? Kate, it's so good to meet you.'

'Likewise,' said Cal, bowing to Kate. He thrust out a hand to Jack. 'Calvin Stern.'

'Jack Logan—Joanna's father.' He turned round, frowning. 'I was about to introduce you to Jo's friend, Isobel James, but—'

'She promised Rufus she'd go straight to the ballroom,' said Jo, wishing she could get the encounter with March behind her.

Kate smiled warmly at Hetty, grateful for the way she'd put them all at ease—other than Jo, who was still as tense as a drawn bow. 'You've come back home to support Rufus?'

'She never needs an excuse to come back to Arnborough, Mrs Logan,' drawled Cal, grinning at his wife.

'I do apologise for Rufus,' said Hetty. 'He's too much on edge about his paintings to even think about good manners.'

'Artistic licence,' said a voice behind them, and Jo's heart turned a somersault in her chest behind the tawny velvet of the dress Kate had forced her to buy.

Everyone turned to face March, who was beckoning over a waiter with a tray of drinks. 'Welcome to Arnborough, everyone,' he said smoothly, and bowed to Kate. 'Mrs Logan— we meet at last.'

She smiled warmly. 'How do you do? What a wonderful, wonderful place you have here. Jo has described it, of course, but the reality of it is breathtaking.'

'My wife is right,' said Jack, shaking March's outstretched hand. 'You must sell a hell of lot of pansies to keep this place going.'

'Pansies?' said Hetty blankly.

'Joanna mistook me for one of the gardeners at the centre the first time we met,' said March suavely. 'How are you, Joanna?'

'Absolutely fine,' she lied. 'How are you?'

'I'm absolutely fine too.'

Hetty smiled brightly on everyone and pressed them to drinks and canapés. 'I really want to hear all about your babies, Kate—may I call you Kate? But once we've had a drink we really must go and look at the paintings. I only hope Rufus doesn't bolt before we get there.'

'Isobel will see that he stays put,' said Jo. 'Is Charlie with him?'

'Yes,' said March. 'He keeps well in the background, but he won't let the star of the show take off.'

The Great Hall, for all its size, was beginning to look so crowded March decided it was time to make for the ballroom. 'I'll leave you to cope in here, Hetty. This way, Mrs Logan.'

'Please call me Kate,' she said, smiling.

'Thank you. I'm grateful for the privilege.'

He was oozing charm from every pore, thought Jo savagely, as she followed behind with Jack.

'Are you really absolutely fine?' asked her father in an undertone.

'Of course I am.'

'That's my girl. Now, tell me,' he added, 'are these paintings any good?'

'Yes. But you know a good thing when you see it, Dad, so judge for yourself.'

The ballroom was packed with people circling round the twelve paintings on display.

'Dad,' said Jo, 'will you join Kate and March? I must find Isobel and have a word with Rufus. And Charlie, too.'

'Coward,' said her father mildly.

'That's me,' she agreed, pulling a face.

Two hours later, when a gratifying number of paintings held red dots to show they were sold, Hetty came to look for Jo to say her parents were ready to leave, then dashed away to see people off.

'Kate needs to get back to the baby,' said Jo, nodding, and eyed Isobel. 'A shame we have to drag you away too.'

'I'm more than ready to be dragged,' said Isobel, and stood firm when Charlie and Rufus protested in unison. 'You're on your way now, Rufus. You're a success. And Charlie will keep your nose to the grindstone to keep you that way.'

'I will,' said Charlie, and kissed Jo's cheek. 'It was good to see you again.' He handed her an envelope. 'Thanks a million, love, but I didn't need it. Hetty put up the money in the end.'

'So all's well that ends well,' said Jo, as she left the ballroom with Isobel—then stiffened as March barred their way.

'Isobel, would you mind telling Jo's parents she'll be along in a minute?' he asked. 'I need a word with her.'

'Of course not.' Isobel ignored the look of panic in Jo's eyes and hurried off.

'Come into the drawing room, Joanna,' said March. 'Please,' he added.

Since the vestibule was crowded with people on their way out, it was impossible to argue. Jo let March usher her into the beautiful, rarely used formality of the drawing room, then turned to face him as he closed the door.

'Have you been ill?' he demanded.

'No.'

'You look—fragile.'

'It's the fashion this season,' she said flippantly, wishing her heart would stop trying to thump a hole in her chest.

'Why did you come tonight?'

'To support Rufus, naturally.'

'Naturally.'

'Look,' she said, edging away, 'I must go. Kate wants to get back to the children and—'

His mouth smothered the rest of her sentence, his arms like iron bands as he pulled her close. At first she tried to fight him, keep her lips closed, but it was a losing battle. And at last, with a broken little sob, she surrendered her mouth to him and let him devour it mercilessly.

When he raised his head at last March was pale but triumphant. She stared at him for a moment, then turned and stormed out of the room, banging the door behind her.

Isobel took one look as she caught up with her, then hurried her outside to Jack's car, thankful that neither of Jo's parents could see her face in the dark interior.

'Sorry about that,' said Jo tightly. 'Lord Arnborough wanted a word.' But he'd wanted—and received, damn him—so much more than that. She blessed her parents' restraint, Isobel's too, when they asked no questions.

Jo's phone rang when she was in bed. She snatched it up, afraid something was wrong with the children, then sat bolt upright when she heard the stomach-clenching tones of Lord Arnborough.

'Joanna?'

'Yes.'

'I hope you weren't asleep.'

'What do you want?'

'It's important I see you. I promise—cross my heart,' he added, 'that I won't pounce on you again, or propose, or do any of those things you take such exception to.'

This, thought Jo, is where I either let my pride take over and say no, or do what I really want to do.

'Are you still there?' he demanded.

'Yes.' She cleared her throat. 'All right, March. Come if you want.'

'Thank you. I'll come to your place after dinner tomorrow—if that's convenient?'

'Yes.'

'Good. I'll see you then. By the way,' he added, 'as well as selling most of his paintings tonight, Rufus got a couple of commissions.'

'How wonderful! Congratulate him for me.'

'I'll do that now. He's off to Italy with Charlie in the morning, so all will be peaceful at Arnborough again. Tomorrow, then, Joanna.'

Jo was ready well ahead of time next evening. She turned on the television, sat staring at it for a while, then turned it off again and picked up a book. After a while she put it down and went to the window, to peer through the darkness at the pouring rain. Then she paced round the room like a caged animal as the minutes dragged slowly past. By nine she was furious. By nine-thirty she was worried sick. At ten, when the phone rang, she seized it—then almost fell apart when it wasn't March.

'Sorry to intrude, Joanna,' said Hetty, 'but is March still with you? He promised to ring me at nine, but he must have forgotten.'

'He never turned up.'

'What? But he set off ages ago. Oh, God!' Hetty heaved in an audible breath. 'Look, Joanna, I'll get off the line in case March is trying to ring you. If he does, tell him to ring me. Please?'

Her voice wavered so much on the last Jo's heart contracted. 'Of course I will— Hang on, Hetty. Someone's ringing my bell.' She ran to the door, phone in hand, and flung it open to find March on her doorstep, soaking wet, bedraggled, and sporting a black eye.

'Sorry I'm late,' he said, shivering.

'For heaven's sake, what happened to you? No, never mind—talk to Hetty first.' Jo thrust her phone at him and closed the door, her heart missing a beat when she heard him tell his sister he'd had a slight accident in the car.

'I'm fine, Hetty, I swear. Cold and wet, but I'm in one piece.' After several more assurances he switched the phone off and handed it back to Jo.

'While you get those wet clothes off, tell me what really happened and I'll put them in the dryer,' she commanded. 'Come into the kitchen.'

March followed her, his shoes squelching along the hall floor. 'A joy-rider in a stolen car shot out of a side road on my way here. I swerved to avoid it. There were sheets of water about, and the E-type doesn't have ABS.'

'What's that?'

'Anti-lock brakes. To my shame, I couldn't control the skid. I went through a hedge and down into a stream.'

'Heavens above, March,' she said in alarm. 'Are you sure you're in one piece?'

'I'll have a shiner tomorrow, plus some bruises, but I'll live.' He toed off his shoes and peeled off his socks. 'If I strip off, can you give me something to cover myself?'

'You need a hot shower first. I'll give you some bath sheets you can drape toga-style afterwards. Best I can do, I'm afraid.'

'Sounds wonderful to me,' he said fervently, following her upstairs. 'The constable who drove me here sat me on a plastic bin bag to save the back seat of his car.'

'Constable? Never mind,' she said hastily. 'Tell me when you come down. Would you like something hot to drink?'

'Not right now. They gave me coffee at the police station. I do apologise,' he said, suddenly formal as he paused in the bathroom doorway. 'This wasn't part of my plan for the evening.'

'No, I don't imagine it was.' Burning to know more about his 'plan', Jo provided him with an armful of towels, waited until he handed his bundle of sodden clothes round the bathroom door, and then left him to it.

When March came downstairs, tastefully draped in crimson towelling, he still looked damp around the edges but a lot better, despite his swelling eye.

Jo met him in the hall. 'Let's go in the parlour.'

When March was settled on the sofa, Jo sat in one of the chairs, leaning forward expectantly. 'Now, tell me about the police bit.'

'The police who'd been in pursuit of the joy-rider locked him in their car, then came to my rescue. They commiserated with me no end when they saw that the E-type was a write-off. My phone didn't survive its ducking, either.' He sighed. 'Another police car was called to take me to the station, where a medical examiner checked me over. After much persuasion he let me off a trip to the local A&E. Then a police car brought me here.' March looked at her for a long minute. 'I should have gone home, I know. But I needed to see you tonight.'

Jo returned the look steadily. 'Why, March?'

He raked a hand through his damp hair, for once looking unsure of himself. 'Because I took one look at you last night and the game was up. I hope to God you still want us to be friends.'

Jo's heart sank. 'Is that what *you* want, March?'

'No,' he said with sudden violence. 'I want to be your husband—as you damn well know. But if you won't go for that, then I'll settle for being your friend, lover—anything you want. I'm so much in love with you, Joanna. I can't sleep, can't concentrate on any damn thing other than wanting to be with you.' His mouth twisted. 'These weeks without you have been utter hell. Hetty's worried about me, and so is Cal. Even Rufus is worried about me—which is a first.' March paused, looking at the motionless figure in the chair. 'Say something, for God's sake,' he said in desperation. 'When a man tells a woman she's his consuming passion he's entitled to *some* reaction.'

Jo got to her feet, surprised her trembling knees managed to hold her up. 'I wish you'd told me that before.'

'What, exactly?' said March, struggling to keep his draperies around him as he got to his feet.

'That you were desperately in love with me, of course.'

He frowned. 'But I did. I have—'

'No. You told me you cared for me, and that I would be the perfect wife to help you run Arnborough. Because I'm so *capable*.'

Because she spat the last out like a dirty word March began to see where he'd gone wrong. 'By day, yes,' he agreed. 'But what I didn't make plain, obviously, is that I'm utterly crazy about you. My bed is a cold and lonely place without you.'

'Mine is like that lately, too,' she said very quietly, and held out her hand. 'You look tired. You need to go to bed.'

'I do. But not because I'm tired,' he said hoarsely.

'Good, because I'm not either.' She gave him a radiant smile. 'Only don't trip over your robes, Caesar.'

March laughed unsteadily, and followed her upstairs as fast as his towels allowed. When they reached her bedroom Jo held up a hand when he tried to remove his draperies and told him to sit on her bed.

'You've had a nasty shock tonight. You need to go slow. I'll do the undressing bit.' By the time the last towel was discarded March was breathing rapidly, his eyes narrowed to fiery gold slits. But Jo's heart hammered for a different reason when she saw his frightening display of bruises.

'Are you sure nothing's broken?' she said, swallowing.

'Absolutely sure,' he said between his teeth. 'If you glance in a southerly direction you'll see that all is in perfect working order.'

To his delight, Jo blushed to the roots of her hair and started removing her clothes in a tearing hurry.

'I thought you were going slow,' he drawled, eyes glued to the process.

'I'm trying, but you're making it hard for me.'

'*I'm* making it hard?' He rolled his eyes and reached for her. 'Come here, my darling. And if you love me don't go *too* slow.'

'I do love you.'

'Say that again?'

'You heard the first time,' she muttered. 'Stop talking and kiss me.'

March pulled her down on his lap and crushed her in his arms as his lips locked on hers. Her plan to go slow evaporated in a steam of desire as his tongue surged between her lips. They both forgot his bruises as he caressed her breasts into taut, quivering life, taking triumphant male pleasure in her choked little moans as he grazed on each nipple in turn, while his hands roamed lower to smooth over her hips and trace a line down her thighs.

She shook her head and pushed his hands away, making a counter-attack with her own as she caressed the long, flat muscles of his back, sliding her hands down his spine to cup the tight, rounded hardness below, her touch delicate to avoid hurting him. He let out a visceral groan of defeat and flipped her on her back to move over her, his lips swallowing her gasp as he thrust home between her thighs to bring them at last to a pleasure which grew so intense as it finally engulfed them that Jo discovered for the first time what the French meant by describing it as 'the little death'.

'How are your bruises?' she asked later, when she had breath enough to speak.

'What bruises?' he murmured into her neck, then raised his head to look down at her, an imperious gleam in his eyes. 'In the unlikely event that you still have any doubts, let me repeat: I love you madly, deeply, every way there is, my beautiful, capable Miss Logan. So, for the last time of asking, will you stop wasting time and marry me?'

'Yes, *please*,' she said fervently.

The six weeks that followed—the shortest possible time, according to the bride's mother, to organise the perfect wedding—were, March complained, the longest of his life.

And to start with there was a major problem. Jack Logan wanted both the service and the reception to take place at Mill House. March, naturally, wanted the wedding in the family church at Arnborough, with guests received in the Great Hall, followed by a wedding breakfast in the ballroom. In which case, he made it plain, he would foot the bill.

'I think the bride should choose where she wants to get married,' Kate told her husband when Jo reported this. 'And we'll fall in with whatever our daughter decides.'

'I suppose you're right. But whichever way she goes,' said Jack flatly, 'I'm the bride's father and I will exercise my privilege to pay.'

Wanting to please both the men she loved, Jo was torn. 'What do you think, Grandpa?'

Tom Logan gave it thought. 'It's only natural that a man whose family has lived in the same house for centuries will want his marriage to take place there. Couldn't you throw a party here when Jo and March come back from honeymoon, Jack? That way you could invite friends and colleagues who wouldn't have expected to go to the actual wedding.'

'Tom,' said Kate, awed, 'that is such a brilliant idea.'

'It might work,' admitted Jack, and looked at Jo. 'What do you think, sweetheart?'

Jo let out the breath she'd been holding. 'I think Grandpa's idea is just wonderful. That way everyone's happy. Aren't they?' she added, eyeing her father.

'Yes,' he said. 'Even me. After all, I'll be walking you down the aisle, whichever one you choose.'

On a cold, bright December day, Joanna Margaret Logan walked down the aisle of St Peter's Church at Arnborough on the arm of her proud, elegant father, smiling at the equally proud, elegant figure of her bridegroom, who stood watching her progress with a look which brought tears to the female eyes in the congregation.

Miss Kitty Logan, wearing the same ethereal ivory chiffon as the bride and chief bridesmaid, walked hand-in-hand with Isobel, her free hand clutching a tiny basket of flowers, with more threaded through her glossy black curls, and caused more surreptitious tears from the mother of the bride and from Mrs Calvin Stern, who gratefully accepted the large white handkerchief offered by her husband.

Jack Logan surrendered his daughter with a kiss, before taking his place by her mother. The Honourable Rufus Clement produced the ring at the exact moment required, to the warm approval of Charlie Peel, seated in the pew behind. And every word was uttered with audible conviction as March Aubrey Clement made his vows to his bride, who returned them in kind.

After much kissing and congratulating in the vestry, the wedding party finally emerged from the church into bracing sunshine to face the battery of photographers waiting to take the money shot of the bride who had captured the eligible Baron Arnborough.

There were shouts on all sides of, 'Look this way, Lady Arnborough.'

She smiled in surprise, and shot a look at the grinning Carey twins in the group of family and friends behind her. 'Gosh—that's me!'

March bent his head to kiss his bride, to the accompaniment of cheers and snapping flashbulbs on all sides. 'It most definitely *is* you,' he assured her, and whispered in her ear, 'But known in private, as I shall prove to you later, as your husband's consuming passion!'

millsandboon.co.uk Community

Join Us!

The Community is the perfect place to meet and chat to kindred spirits who love books and reading as much as you do, but it's also the place to:

- **Get the inside scoop from authors about their latest books**
- **Learn how to write a romance book with advice from our editors**
- **Help us to continue publishing the best in women's fiction**
- **Share your thoughts on the books we publish**
- **Befriend other users**

Forums: Interact with each other as well as authors, editors and a whole host of other users worldwide.

Blogs: Every registered community member has their own blog to tell the world what they're up to and what's on their mind.

Book Challenge: We're aiming to read 5,000 books and have joined forces with The Reading Agency in our inaugural Book Challenge.

Profile Page: Showcase yourself and keep a record of your recent community activity.

Social Networking: We've added buttons at the end of every post to share via digg, Facebook, Google, Yahoo, technorati and de.licio.us.

www.millsandboon.co.uk

2 FREE BOOKS
AND A SURPRISE GIFT

We would like to take this opportunity to thank you for reading this Mills & Boon® book by offering you the chance to take TWO more specially selected books from the Modern™ series absolutely FREE! We're also making this offer to introduce you to the benefits of the Mills & Boon® Book Club™—

- **FREE home delivery**
- **FREE gifts and competitions**
- **FREE monthly Newsletter**
- **Exclusive Mills & Boon Book Club offers**
- **Books available before they're in the shops**

Accepting these FREE books and gift places you under no obligation to buy, you may cancel at any time, even after receiving your free books. Simply complete your details below and return the entire page to the address below. You don't even need a stamp!

YES Please send me 2 free Modern books and a surprise gift. I understand that unless you hear from me, I will receive 4 superb new books every month for just £3.19 each, postage and packing free. I am under no obligation to purchase any books and may cancel my subscription at any time. The free books and gift will be mine to keep in any case.

Ms/Mrs/Miss/Mr_____ Initials _____

Surname _____
Address _____

_____ Postcode _____

Send this whole page to: Mills & Boon Book Club, Free Book Offer, FREEPOST NAT 10298, Richmond, TW9 1BR